# A Not So Shocking Murder

Holt Jacobs Mystery - Book 1

Lily Stirling

Copyright © 2023 by Lily Stirling

All rights reserved.

No part of this publication may be reproduced, distributed, or transmitted in any form or by any means, including photocopying, recording, or other electronic or mechanical methods, without the prior written permission of the publisher, except as permitted by U.S. copyright law.

The story, all names, characters, and incidents portrayed in this production are fictitious. No identification with actual persons (living or deceased), places, buildings, and products is intended or should be inferred.

Cover Design by Mariah Sinclair

*~ Dedicated to my drivers ~*
*Bryan, Eric, Jim, Justin, Mike, Rick, Sean, Taylor, & Tim*

# Contents

| | |
|---|---:|
| CHAPTER 1 | 1 |
| CHAPTER 2 | 10 |
| CHAPTER 3 | 21 |
| CHAPTER 4 | 31 |
| CHAPTER 5 | 40 |
| CHAPTER 6 | 50 |
| CHAPTER 7 | 58 |
| CHAPTER 8 | 69 |
| CHAPTER 9 | 77 |
| CHAPTER 10 | 84 |
| CHAPTER 11 | 95 |
| CHAPTER 12 | 105 |
| CHAPTER 13 | 115 |
| CHAPTER 14 | 121 |
| CHAPTER 15 | 133 |
| CHAPTER 16 | 138 |
| CHAPTER 17 | 146 |
| CHAPTER 18 | 155 |

| | |
|---|---|
| CHAPTER 19 | 165 |
| CHAPTER 20 | 174 |
| CHAPTER 21 | 180 |
| SEATTLE | 183 |
| Congratulations! | 188 |
| About the Author | 190 |
| Acknowledgments | 191 |

# CHAPTER 1

A seahorse was ogling me. Its marble eyes were peering straight into my soul. What kind of tourist trap was seahorse themed?

"Holt," Mom said from the other side of Dad. "We're inside. Take off the sunglasses."

"Uh-oh," my baby sister, Juniper, said. She was the only one at the booth who noticed (or cared) I was in trouble. Her husband, Jude, was too busy on his phone, while my other sister, Casey, and her husband, Nigel, were too busy with their kids.

I cleared my throat, considering my sunglass options. Either I would inconvenience Mom or make my headache worse. Dad shifted in his spot between us, but he needn't have worried. After a lifetime of battles with the self-proclaimed smartest woman in the world, I knew this wasn't a hill worth dying on.

When I removed my shades, the pounding between my temples intensified. Just great.

"I didn't know you had green eyes," Juniper said loud enough that everyone at the table began staring.

I love my family. Don't get me wrong. Family is great. Which is why I spent Christmas with them, then Valentine's Day for Juniper's wedding. Now Mother's Day? Three trips in six months was pushing it.

After everyone at the table had stopped staring, I was still being watched by that taxidermied seahorse. I stared back at the creepy critter. It was that or pay attention to Casey asking Mom if finger painting was scheduled during Harper and Baxter's nap time.

I blinked, losing the stare-off, then blinked a few more times to rest up for round two of the Holt versus Seahorse stare-off.

I'm usually not this crazy, I swear. I'd be in much better shape if my flight hadn't been delayed six times before being one long ride of turbulence. Or if the foldout bed in my room above the garage hadn't been a medieval torture device. Or—and here's the real kicker—if Mom hadn't dragged me out of bed for a sunrise hike with no access to coffee or caffeine of any kind until lunch at a weird seahorse diner.

Mom was telling Casey that finger painting on the pier was after naps as I locked into round two. Her announcing "Holt and I are scheduled for mother-son bonding during nap time" nearly cost me the game. But I'm a professional. That seahorse was going down.

Remember that sunrise hike? Well, Casey and Nigel didn't go because of Harper and Baxter's sleep schedule. No one told me watching the sunrise was optional. Mom had saved that little nugget until after Dad had begun to drive. Sure Harper and Baxter were little kids, but they got to sleep in and take naps?

Even though the caffeine headache was from Mom's poor planning, I removed my sunglasses without an argument. But if Mom expected me to stay awake all afternoon, she had another thing coming. Ideally, I'd lie down in my garret above the garage. But if I was forced to climb aboard the family fun bus, I would be conking out in the van. Better the van than nodding off into a puddle of finger paints.

My eyes were drying out, but the tiredness helped keep me alive in the stare-off. I was about to blink when a miracle happened. The seahorse blinked. There's a slight chance this was sleep deprivation and blinding headache talking, but the seahorse blinked at me. We were tied 1–1. Sitting up a little straighter, I was preparing myself for the tiebreaker when a white-haired dude took a seat by the register. He blocked the seahorse and disqualified my competitor. I was the default winner.

I could have picked a new seahorse to stare at. I mean, the place was called The Dining Seahorse. But the other seahorses I'd spotted were plastic toys or stuffed animals. Well, that's if you didn't count all the cartoon seahorses peering from menus and signs and swimming in the coloring pages given to my niece and nephew. The coloring pages were wasted on them. Baxter rarely colored within the lines, while with Harper, it was a win anytime the crayon connected with the paper.

Beyond not loving any of the other seahorses, my bond with the taxidermied seahorse had been built on convenience. He'd been in my eyeline. My gaze didn't shift, but the view had changed to the back of the dude who'd ruined my game. He wore a bright blue T-shirt covered in sponsors proclaiming he was a 10K finisher.

I couldn't judge. I was wearing a mint-green T-shirt with OUR AWESOME JACOBS FAMILY VACAY printed on the front. The shirts were mandatory, a uniform of sorts. Everyone was wearing one, from my parents to my sisters, their husbands, and Casey's two kids. Not only did the shirt wash out my mostly natural tan, but it made my family look disgustingly more touristy than all the other tourists congregating in the tourist trap town known as Amelia's Haven, Oregon. I hated it. And I *wanted* to hate the Pacific Ocean for summoning us. But it wasn't the Pacific Ocean's fault; it was my mom's.

Harper began making unintelligible squawking sounds as she waved the seahorse coloring page at us. Juniper was positively gushing, while Mom and Dad were suitably impressed.

Unfortunately, Harper continued making sounds and waving the picture. It did not help my headache.

"You want Uncle Holt to see your picture?" Casey asked.

I forced my mouth into something resembling a smile as I analyzed the random scribbles over the printed seahorses. "Wow," I said. Harper kept waving the picture. Was I still on the hook? "Um, you used a lot of blue…That's a good color."

Thankfully, that satisfied her, and I could return to my coffee. What a way to spend a vacation.

Juniper had jumped at a free trip, calling it a second honeymoon, and Casey was too family oriented to say no. I declined. Multiple times. Then Mom and Juniper began a targeted attack to get me to come. What finally had me buying a ticket was Mom saying it could be the last time we'd all be together as a family. Mom would absolutely drag us to the same location so we could hear bad news at the same time. So I'd agreed and had spent the whole morning waiting for my parents to make an announcement that would shatter life as I knew it.

So far, nothing. For instance, instead of impending doom, Casey and Mom had returned to talking about finger painting. Why?

I took a long gulp of my fourth cup of coffee. I was doing my absolute best to make up for lost time. At my request, the teenage waitress had left the pot at our booth, and I was drinking as much as possible.

Baxter disappeared under the table, chasing a french fry or crayon. "Careful," Mom was saying right as Baxter headbutted my legs. My half-full cup of coffee spilled down my shirt. The coffee was hotter than comfortable but not exactly scalding. The real damage was to my mint *vacay* shirt.

Nigel began apologizing for his kid while telling Baxter to apologize, all while Casey told him not to eat french fries off the floor. Instead of yelling, I nodded like the understanding uncle everyone knew I was. Really, all I cared about was getting to the bathroom, where I could survey the damage in peace.

With Mom worried I'd make a getaway, I'd been wedged in the middle of the wraparound booth. I had to wait for Juniper and Jude to slide out before I could head to the bathroom to try getting cleaned up.

"Was that on purpose?" Juniper whispered. "We all know you hate the shirt." I gave her an older-brother glare before stalking away.

I was passing the register right as a short guy in a cheap suit and a man and woman in EMT uniforms were paying. Which begged the question: Did locals actually eat at The Dining Seahorse? The decor was nightmare fuel. The food was not only greasy but tasted like old grease.

The female EMT's shiny black ponytail caught my attention as I passed, and I stumbled into the white-haired Mr. FunRun, who'd ruined my stare-off. It pushed him against his cup of sweet tea. The glass bobbled, threatening to be the second spill in five minutes.

"Watch it!" someone called.

"Sorry," I said to Mr. FunRun. "You good?"

Mr. FunRun steadied the cup before nodding and waving me off. I made it to the bathroom without further mishaps. I should have felt worse about tripping into Mr. FunRun, but I was still salty about him stealing my seahorse friend.

The bathroom was single occupancy, and I let out a deep breath once I was safely locked inside. A fan hummed in the background, but the room was relatively dark and quiet compared to the madhouse beyond. It was nice no one could barge in and find me shirtless by the sink.

I took my time rinsing the coffee from the shirt before adding soap from a seahorse-shaped dispenser and scrubbing. Juniper's question replayed in my head. Had I wrecked the shirt on purpose?

The coffee stain washed from a dark brown to a light tan. The mint-colored shirt now had a strange camo pattern. I eyed the dripping shirt. We were at a beach. How did The Dining Seahorse feel about shirtless clientele? Would the teenagers working in the restaurant really care? Then I remembered Mom was the only reason I was at the stupid restaurant. If the staff didn't yell at me, Mom would.

After wringing it out, I held it under the hand dryer. Five minutes later, it was still damp, but I wriggled into it.

Checking my reflection was a bad idea. Why had no one mentioned I was walking around town with the non-sexy version of bedhead? My normally styled blondish hair was a curly mess. The set of my jaw and the tension in my eyes showed just how irritated I was. Definitely not flattering. I should have insisted on showering before sunrise.

I washed my face and did what I could to my hair with water and finger-combing. It wasn't great, but I no longer looked like I'd just rolled out of bed. At least my vacation stubble was growing in nicely.

Unfortunately, I ran out of things to do. I needed to rejoin my family. My hand paused on the door as I geared up to leave my fortress of solitude. Taking one last look at the seahorse soap dispenser, I exited.

My progress from the little boys' room was slowed by the restaurant's newest patron entering the walkway right in front of me. She was my age but had the dress sense of an eccentric great-aunt. Everything about her was too much. The red hair was overstyled, the perfume too strong, and the dress was covered with bright orange-yellow apricots. She paused to greet almost every table with a hello and a beaming smile. Miss Apricots wasn't large, but she somehow filled the aisle, so I couldn't get past her. I was trapped and stuck eavesdropping on all her little pleasantries. A charming combination that made my day that much worse. Was anyone glad to see her? I couldn't tell. Miss Apricots even waved at Mom before sitting on the stool beside Mr. FunRun.

At last I could sit at our booth, and I slid in at the end. Everyone was done eating, but I had no clue when we'd be leaving.

Juniper leaned over Jude to whisper, "I thought you'd made a run for it."

"Not without my sunglasses."

She passed me a fresh cup of coffee, and I kept an eye on Baxter and any under-the-table antics. The caffeine had eased some of the tension in my head, but what I really needed was a nap.

My eyes were beginning to glaze as I refocused on the blue 10K finisher shirt. Mr. FunRun and Miss Apricots were a strange pair. He was at least twice her age and dressed way more casually. They leaned toward each other and talked in low tones. Miss Apricots never lost her fake smile, while Mr. FunRun's face grew red, and sweat formed on his temples.

"Holt!" Mom called.

Juniper twisted over Jude again. "Pay attention."

"What?" I sounded cranky.

"Are you ready to leave?" Mom asked.

I nodded. I'd been ready to leave since we'd arrived.

Putting on my sunglasses, I almost ran into Mr. FunRun for the second time as he stumbled off the stool. His face was really red, and he was coughing. Miss Apricots's smile had slipped as she said, "Allen? Allen, are you all right?"

I don't know what came over me. I'm an engineer, not a doctor.

"Is he choking?" I asked.

Miss Apricots shook her head. If the answer were yes, what would I have done? Googled the Heimlich?

"Any allergies?"

The man shook his head, still coughing.

"Heart condition? Is there a medical bracelet?"

Whatever TV-show doctor I was impersonating was having an off day. The man gave a violent shudder and fell into Miss Apricots's arms.

The waitress dropped her coffeepot. "Oh, Dakota. Not again!"

Where had my mother dragged me?

# CHAPTER 2

Miss Apricots stumbled under the weight, and I helped lower Mr. FunRun to the ground before they toppled over. I tried to remember the basics from my lapsed first aid certification. I couldn't find a pulse and began performing CPR—right beside a floor mural of another seahorse.

The world shrank to counting chest compressions and rescue breaths. Staring down at my hands, I saw the race logo on his shirt. It was for Seattle's Rainy Days 10K. Wasn't that the race I'd done last June? I tried to ignore the shirt, but it was right there. Something about it—us running the same race—bothered me.

Mom called 911 during my McSteamy impression. But I was too busy counting compressions to understand why a hand was on my shoulder.

"We'll take it from here." The voice cut my focus enough for me to notice the paramedic uniform.

I tried to stand, but my knees buckled from kneeling for so long, and I ended up crawling out of the way. Staying on the floor, I stretched my legs out and leaned against a booth. The EMTs loaded the guy onto a stretcher and rushed him away. It wouldn't matter. While I'd done CPR until they'd come, it was useless. He was dead the moment he fell into Miss Apricots's arms.

The rush of adrenaline was wearing off. At first, trying to keep myself from visibly shaking took all my concentration. Then I noticed the seahorse from the floor mural judging me. Like it could have performed CPR better? I moved one of my legs to cover its eyes. This was such an improvement, I was able to take stock of my surroundings.

Mom was seated above me at the random booth. Her hand was wrapped securely around the back of my neck. For some reason, that had calmed me as a child. I must be in rough shape for her to pull out the big guns.

Cops had scattered throughout the diner. Yellow crime scene tape had appeared and was stretched across certain areas. Mom's hand tightened, and she gestured to where Miss Apricots was talking to a man who was shorter than her. He wasn't wearing a police uniform, but a shiny badge glinted on his belt. This was the detective, dressed in a cheap suit and shoes that didn't match his belt.

Short? Cheap suit? He was the guy paying at the register. One of the locals, crazy enough to eat here. The guy was built like a tank. He had neck muscles. Only bodybuilders have neck muscles. Did he work out so much to compensate for being five foot five?

Miss Apricots faced him head-on as they spoke, leaving no space between their bodies. At one point, his hand brushed her arm. The redhead said something to the cop, and they both looked at me. Completely stuck, I stared back. Even Mom squeezing my neck didn't break the trance. They knew I'd been watching, and I still couldn't look away.

The cop said something to Miss Apricots. Mom let go of my neck as he strode over to stand above me. I was still sitting on the floor. Even then, the detective, neck muscles and all, wasn't very imposing.

It's inappropriate. I know it's inappropriate. A man had just died. Maybe it was shock talking. But the detective was strutting around like an arrogant rooster. And it took all I had not to burst out laughing.

"You are?" he asked.

"Holt Jacobs."

I extended my hand. Instead of shaking it, he grabbed the hand and hauled me to my feet. At six one, I towered over him. His eyes widened, and I smirked.

He quickly recovered and became all business. "I'm Detective Reynolds. I'll be taking your statement regarding the death."

While I heard him, it was hard to process the words. There was so much noise. Cops were talking, customers were talking, and there was the clink of dishes from people who continued eating. Why let a dead body ruin lunch?

"Did you hear me?" His voice was more forceful.

Breaking eye contact with yet another seahorse, I tried to focus. "Yeah?"

The detective huffed—like I was the worst part of his day. "Can you tell me what happened?"

Crying cut through the clatter. Where was that coming from? It was Harper. Then Nigel was trying to get Baxter to stop squeezing her while Casey shushed everyone.

"Holt Jacobs!"

"Hm?"

# A NOT SO SHOCKING MURDER 13

The cop opened and closed his mouth a couple of times, unable to find the right words. Miss Apricots came to his side and asked, "Should he be checked out?"

He eyed her. "Really, you both should be. It was quite a shock."

She tossed her hair back. "I'm used to it."

The detective watched her a little longer before sizing me up. I was swaying side to side, finding it difficult to balance. "Fine. I'll make sure the ambulance comes back."

He began talking into his radio, the words blending into the clamor. The clinking of glass was added to the madness as the waitress began sweeping up the broken coffeepot.

"Fresh air?" Miss Apricots suggested.

The cop said something under his breath before ushering Miss Apricots and me to the exit. The patrol officer guarding the door let us pass outside, and I was finally free of seahorses. Clouds were growing denser overhead. The temperature was in that awkward spot where you couldn't decide on whether or not you needed a jacket. A gust of wind had me shivering in my damp shirt. At least it was quieter. I'd take distant waves over diner noise any day. Inhaling deeply, I did my best to channel the stuff Juniper went on about, like centering myself.

"That's better," Miss Apricots said.

Giving a curt nod, the cop left her at one bench before leading me to another. He took a deep breath. Was he centering too? "So, Holt. What happened?"

"The guy tripped into me, then I heard Miss Apricots...ur...um, her—"

"Dakota," he said, unimpressed with the nickname.

"Sure. I heard, uh…" For a moment, I totally blanked on her name. "Dakota?"

He nodded.

"Dakota's voice got loud. She was asking what was wrong. I went to help. The guy lost consciousness, and I performed CPR until the ambulance came."

The cop blinked. "That's a workout."

My mouth twitched. "I did what I could."

"Right, right." My detective friend squared his shoulders. "But, like, I lift regularly, and having to squat, bent over for, say, ten minutes compressing someone's chest, it's more than most would do."

"Okay."

I couldn't tell if I was being made fun of. Nothing was making sense.

"Did you notice anything in particular?" he asked.

The greasy food had given me acid reflux, and I cleared my throat before answering. "I don't know…There's a tacky amount of seahorses in there."

"It is called The Dining Seahorse."

"It's not tacky?"

The detective pressed his lips into a thin line. "Right. Anything else?"

Trying to reach through the blur of memories to a solitary moment, I said the only thing I could think of. "Kids are loud."

"Fine," he said. "Thank you for your time. The paramedics will get you looked at."

The ambulance was pulling into the parking lot, and my cop went to meet it. Once it parked, the passenger door opened, and a paunchy EMT in his forties appeared. He was the kind of guy you'd expect to see lounging in a lawn chair during a kids' soccer game. Soccer Dad spoke to my detective friend before coming my way.

"Sir, if you would come with me," he said, leading me to the back of the ambulance.

As I followed, I remembered Mom had taught me to avoid following strangers into the back of vans. Was this the exception that proved the rule?

Halfway up the first step, I hesitated. Was I about to sit on a dead man's bed?

"We changed the sheets," Soccer Dad said.

Well, if they changed the sheets…

Sitting on the bed, I was finally somewhere dim and quiet.

"Are you cold?" the guy asked, with sweat around his temples.

I was shivering. "Um, maybe."

He opened an emergency blanket that was basically a huge sheet of aluminum foil and wrapped it around my shoulders. I can say this about getting in the back of vans. The service was top-notch. Real five-star experience.

"Sit tight," Soccer Dad said before going outside.

A woman's voice at the front of the ambulance caught my attention. "I know. I'm sorry. I called as soon as it happened…" There was a pause. She must be on the phone. "All right. I have to go. Bye."

The driver's door opened and shut; then Soccer Dad's voice drifted in through the open back door. "…of a formality. I'll check Dakota."

The woman's voice replied, "You're sure?"

"It's best for everyone."

"Okay," she said.

Now, I don't know what was shock over doing CPR on a dead man versus sleep deprivation mixed with a caffeine overload. But I was unraveling in the ambulance and hugged the shock blanket closer without even knowing if I was cold.

"Hello. Can you tell me your name?"

I didn't notice her enter. My previous medic had been replaced by an extremely hot woman with black hair and brown eyes. And that ponytail. Had she been paying at the diner, or was I hallucinating?

All that came out of my mouth was "Uhhh."

Was this shock?

She sat across from me. "Let's do an easier question. Do you know what day it is?"

I was about to answer when she leaned closer with a flashlight in her hand. She smelled really good. I needed to remember what day it was. But her scent was muddling my brain. This wasn't happening.

*I'm a college-educated engineer. I should be able to answer a simple question.*

"Tuesday! It's Tuesday," I said, panicking.

She nodded before shining a light in my eyes. "Very good."

"And it's Jacobs, Holt Jacobs…um…" Was I introducing myself like James Bond? I needed to clarify. "Just Holt."

She smiled.

I burped.

No, burped is too civilized. A belch emerged from the pit of my stomach, carrying the stench of coffee and grease, blowing right into her face. She recoiled, and I blathered so many apologies I sounded drunk.

"Don't worry." Her mouth quirked like she was trying not to smile. She placed a small gadget on my finger. "It's a hazard of the job. You wouldn't believe how many college kids have puked all over me."

"Really? For me, puking is more of a second-date thing." Was I the guy hitting on the EMT? Super original.

She ignored the remark. "Your heart rate is elevated."

Wouldn't be if Soccer Dad did the examination.

"What have you had to drink?"

"Coffee."

She nodded. "Any water?"

"Um…" My day needs to start with coffee. Had I bothered with water? The whole morning swirled together, ending with Mr. FunRun lying dead by a mosaic of a grinning seahorse. Stupid, ugly seahorse. "That guy really just—"

"Died? Yes." Her brown eyes met mine, and they were soft with understanding.

Running a hand through my hair, I refocused on the original question. "I don't know if I've had water. Mom had me up at sunrise and didn't schedule coffee until lunch. I'm so used to coffee in the morning, I don't think I had anything else."

"You're dehydrated."

I frowned. "There was plenty of coffee at lunch."

Her lips twitched. "It's still a good idea to drink water."

"Makes sense." Then I hiccuped. I was transforming into an alcoholic bum in an old movie. Was my nose red? That would truly complete the ensemble.

"Okay. I'll release you, but you need to rest and hydrate."

"Would you do me a favor?" I leaned toward her, swaying closer than intended, and almost fell into her lap.

She stiffened. "Maybe."

My eyes widened, and I pulled back. Had she thought I was trying to ask her out? "Not that…I, uh, no—right? Obviously, 'cause…anyway."

Her eyes twinkled. Was she trying not to laugh? "What did you want?"

"If I'm supposed to rest, can you give my mom a doctor's note or something to get me out of finger painting on the pier?"

Was that the second time I'd brought up my mother? I'm usually a lot smoother.

"You're trying to get out of finger painting?" Her mouth quirked up. Hopefully she found all the talk of Mom endearing and not pathetic.

"Embarrassing to admit, but my finger painting isn't as good as I'd like." I fought a yawn, a wave of exhaustion hitting me. The shivering had stopped, and I was beginning to relax. Was my EMT magic?

She nodded. Understanding or pretending to understand. "I'll let your mother know you'll be taking the afternoon off."

"Really?"

"Yeah. I don't want to be called to the pier for a dehydrated tourist passed out in a puddle of finger paint."

"What makes you think I'm a tourist?"

She pointed at my damp, coffee-stained vacay shirt.

Have I mentioned I hate this shirt?

True to her word, she marched over to where my family was grouped in their matching vacay shirts and pulled my mom aside. What were the chances the EMT would convince Mom to change the schedule?

I couldn't hear what she said. Dad and Juniper went to either side of me and led me to the nine-passenger van.

Casey and Nigel had already loaded up their kids. Harper and Baxter had gotten weepy, which was explained as being overtired. If I started shrieking, would I get the same sympathy?

"Just a little longer," Casey was saying. "Once Grandma comes, we can go."

Baxter said something unintelligible, and Nigel replied. Had Nigel understood?

We were all waiting for Mom to finish talking. When Mom arrived, she didn't talk about the schedule but grabbed a water bottle from the cooler and made me drink it while Dad drove back to the rental. I finished the bottle as Dad turned into the driveway, and Mom was waiting with a new bottle. She still hadn't said if she'd changed her mind, so I took the water bottle without any argument and began drinking.

Once Dad parked, I attempted to join the mass exodus and sneak away to my room. "Wait a minute, Holt."

I stayed. Though I don't know if it was out of respect or fear. To my surprise, Juniper also stayed, letting Jude go on without her. Juniper and I sat in the front row, while Mom twisted around in the shotgun seat to face us. Mom was in a tough spot. Either she'd have to rearrange her day based on the advice of a stranger or pretend to have fun with a cranky son for the sake of the precious schedule.

"It was brought to my attention you could use some quiet." She sighed. "The schedule's tight, and if we cancel this afternoon's bonding time, there isn't another place we could put it."

Is there a polite way of saying, *I'd prefer a date with my pillow than with you?* If there were, I couldn't come up with it.

"We could trade," Juniper suggested.

We both looked at her.

"I take Holt's slot today, and he takes mine tomorrow."

Mom considered this. "I wouldn't change the activities. Juniper, I'd expect you to go rock climbing."

Juniper smiled. "Sounds great."

Mom nodded slowly as she mentally fixed the calendar in her head. "All right, Juniper. Let's meet back here in five. Wear proper shoes."

Juniper's smile grew. "Sure thing."

As soon as Mom left the van, I sagged against the seat.

"You owe me," Juniper said, poking a finger in my face. "And if I break a nail rock climbing, you're paying for my manicure."

I shrugged. "Whatever."

"Not a thank-you, but I'll take it."

We were this close to my room, and I was tempted to fall asleep in the van. Getting up, walking through the garage (with all its garage smells), and going upstairs would take so much effort. What got me in gear was the fear Mom would change her mind if she saw me again.

While the rest of my family had gone into the vacation home, I had to walk across the driveway to enter the detached garage and go up the plywood staircase to get to my tiny apartment. Ignoring the foldout bed, I collapsed on the leather couch. Managing to take off my damp vacay shirt, I tossed it away. I didn't bother closing the curtains.

I would sound like a better person if, once I actually lay down, I was unable to sleep, tortured with thoughts of death. That would be a total lie. My heart was beating fast with all the caffeine, but I passed out the second I closed my eyes.

# CHAPTER 3

Someone was shaking me.

"No," I grumbled.

"Come on, wake up." It was Juniper.

"Get Dad to drive you."

Juniper giggled. "We're both in our twenties. Wait, aren't you pushing thirty?"

Cute, Juniper. Real cute.

At this point I was awake enough to know I wasn't a teenager being woken by his bratty little sister with orders to take her to the mall. Which begged the question, what was she up to?

"What are you doing?" I tried to hug blankets around myself, and instead of blankets found my bare chest had sealed onto the leather couch.

"I'm your alarm clock or fairy godmother. Whichever you prefer." She stood there, annoyingly perfect. Juniper claimed to make a living being a social media influencer. I never followed her. There are things a man should never learn about his sister—knowing if she'd eaten a Tide Pod is one of them. Whether or not she was successful, she always managed to look airbrushed. Even in a messy bun and sweats, she gave the impression she was off to a photo shoot.

Grimacing, I peeled myself off the couch and sat up. "How did you get in?"

"You didn't even close the door."

Oh.

Trying to smooth out my hair, I asked, "Please tell me I dreamed about a dead guy in a creepy diner."

"His name was Allen, and it was The Dining Seahorse."

So it was real. Fantastic. Though that meant the medic was also real. I'd burped and hiccuped into her face, almost fallen into her, and asked her to tell my mommy I needed a nap. Could there be a worst first impression? At least I was on vacation. I would never see her again. That should have been a consolation, but I still dry heaved.

"If you're going to barf, use this." Juniper stood ready with a garbage can.

"You're a little overeager," I muttered, rubbing my temples.

She shrugged. "Mom sent me on a mission to tell you we're all meeting by the van in half an hour for supper."

Was she talking about food? I glared up at her. "We just ate lunch."

Juniper popped her hip and crossed her arms. "We ate five hours ago."

How long had I been sleeping?

Reading my mind, Juniper added ever so helpfully, "Harper and Baxter take shorter naps than you."

"Harper and Baxter weren't forced out of bed before sunrise."

"I was up at sunrise, and you don't see me whining about it."

"Must mean you're perfect," I said, settling back into the couch.

Juniper began tugging at my arm. "Come on."

I cracked an eye open. "Any way out of this?"

"You missed finger painting and your mother-child bonding time. You miss dinner, and Mom will haunt you."

I frowned. "Is that it? Mom's dying? Is that why she's dragged us all to the beach?"

"What? No!" Juniper paused. "I don't know. It was a joke. Is there something wrong with Mom?"

"You didn't find it suspicious Mom insisted we all take off work to spend the week of Mother's Day together?"

Juniper shrugged. "I don't question paid vacations."

"Why would she drag us all to a sand shack if she or Dad weren't sick or"—I nodded—"you know…"

"I know?"

"Separating."

Juniper scrunched her nose. "Separating?"

"From each other."

Juniper threw a pillow at my face. Real mature.

"Don't be stupid," she said. "We were all together for Christmas and then at my wedding. You remember? On Valentine's Day. I wore a white dress. Jude wore a tux."

How could I forget my sister's Valentine's wedding? There were red roses, pink bridesmaids, and Baxter dressed as Cupid, shirtless with a bow and wedding rings tied to an arrow. Then, for the reception, Juniper danced with Dad to "Jennifer Juniper," the song she was named after. It was all so…cute.

"Do you want me to dry heave again?"

Another pillow came my way. "Shut up."

"Do you really expect our parents to say on Christmas or your wedding, *Hey kids, our marriage is kaput*? And if one of them's sick, they may have just gotten diagnosed."

Juniper sat beside me. "You might be right."

"Thank you," I said, ever so modestly.

"I said *might*, Your Majesty. That doesn't mean you're right." Juniper's eyes lit up. "Is this why you've been a butt?"

"What did you call me?"

"A butt, who's been rude and sulky all day."

"I was going for brooding and mysterious."

"Try harder." We sat in silence until Juniper brightened with a new idea. "Maybe they won the lottery and are bringing us here to tell us we're millionaires."

"When have Mom or Dad ever bought lottery tickets?"

"Well, it could be a distant relative who made their money in oil shares, and they died, leaving us a massive inheritance."

I sighed and tried fixing my hair. "Yeah, that's probably it."

"If there's a big announcement coming, I'm betting Mom will give it at Saturday's fancy dinner." She shrugged. "Or the Mother's Day brunch."

Would they leave me in suspense for the whole week?

Juniper tugged on my arm. "Now, are you staying in your room for the night and risking eternal haunting, or are you going to shower and meet us at the van?"

I raised my eyebrows. "Shower?"

"Yeah, you kind of stink."

"Thanks, sis. Love you too."

"Hey, at least Mom didn't send Casey."

She had a point. Casey would have arrived with Harper on her hip and Baxter running around her legs, making the whole place a zoo.

"I don't want to be haunted," I said, standing.

Juniper didn't get up. I looked from her to the door. She didn't move.

"Now get out."

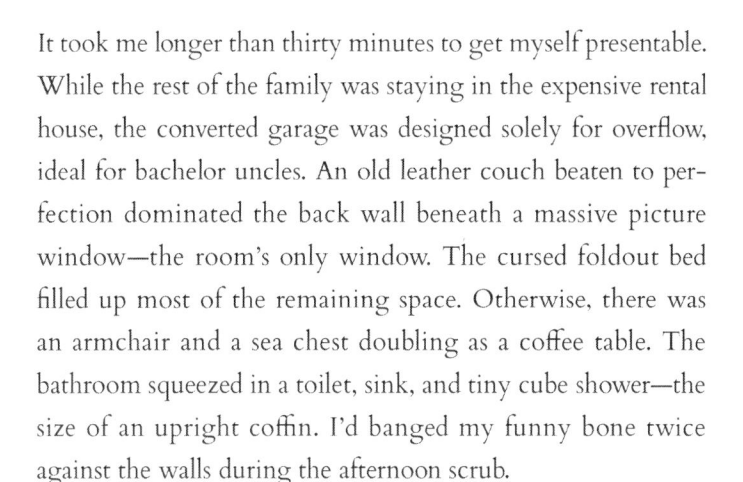

---

It took me longer than thirty minutes to get myself presentable. While the rest of the family was staying in the expensive rental house, the converted garage was designed solely for overflow, ideal for bachelor uncles. An old leather couch beaten to perfection dominated the back wall beneath a massive picture window—the room's only window. The cursed foldout bed filled up most of the remaining space. Otherwise, there was an armchair and a sea chest doubling as a coffee table. The bathroom squeezed in a toilet, sink, and tiny cube shower—the size of an upright coffin. I'd banged my funny bone twice against the walls during the afternoon scrub.

Putting on a half-zip pullover that wasn't a mass-produced poly-cotton blend was the highlight of my day. Next, I combed product through my damp hair. I was already late, but there was one last thing I needed to do. The squeaky folding bed that had been dumpster-dived from a 1950s hospital was folded up and shoved into the darkest corner, since burning it in effigy might be rude…and illegal.

Lucky for me, Casey and her family arrived even later. If I'd been last, Mom would have lectured me about respecting people's time. As it was, all Harper had to do was grin and call, "Gamma!" and Mom was all smiles.

Ideally, we'd eat somewhere that served something other than deep-fried seafood. Maybe I was becoming an old man, but what I wanted more than anything was a good bowl of chicken noodle soup and some saltines.

"Where are we eating?" I asked when we were all loaded in the van.

"At water-horsey!" Baxter yelled.

It took all of my loving-uncle strength to keep from twisting around to Baxter's car seat and yelling, *Not on your life.* Good thing I'm a loving uncle.

Mom spoke up, "It says on the itinerary."

I blinked. Did anyone actually think I read that?

Juniper gave me a look like she was a superhero. "Do you know what food The Marina serves?"

"They're famous for their clam chowder," Mom said while I grimaced. "Beyond that, they have the usual. Crab, shrimp, fish, and chips."

My stomach gurgled.

After lunch, I couldn't do another meal of fried food. Even the clam chowder sounded too rich. Choosing to be a brat, Juniper said, "Yum," as my face turned the shade of the dead guy.

When we arrived, it became clear The Marina was split into two very different spaces. Nearer the beach was a mega-stocked outdoor bar, while we headed inside for the family dining option. The decor, while less atrocious than the water-horsey dive, was pretty bold. At best the ambience was eclectic. Colored lights hung along the ceiling, a couple of sizes larger than your average Christmas lights, while the walls were covered with photos and fishing junk.

"Did you want this seat?" Nigel asked, half rising.

What? I'd been standing right next to Nigel's spot at the table, gazing wistfully at the outdoor bar. "No, sorry. Thanks." I moved to the empty chair at the end of the table and sat down. Casey pursed her lips and shook her head. She would have said something, but with Baxter prone to repeat things, she kept silent—I knew there was a reason I liked that kid.

In the end, while I didn't get the world's best bowl of chicken soup, it was better than the canned stuff and much better than the clam chowder everyone else was digging into.

Juniper had been way off when she said I'd been a sulky butt the entire day. However, I hadn't exactly been the most sociable. So I ordered a ginger ale and did my best to smile.

I was drinking my second refill when I saw Miss Apricots (or Dakota) come in and stand by the pickup station. Mom also saw her. "Dakota!"

Oh no. Mom was on a first-name basis with her? This could only end disastrously.

Dakota's overdone smile was back, and she took a step toward our table.

"Come on, sit down. There's an empty seat next to Holt—the single one." Mom widened her eyes, and I wanted to disappear into a puddle of goo.

While I had a lifetime of experience dealing with my mother, Dakota was stuck doing what most people did—freezing—before going along with whatever my mom wanted. "Uh, okay." Miss Apricots sat beside me. From this angle, I saw she wasn't just wearing an apricot dress but also had apricot earrings.

I flashed her a winning grin. "Hello," I said, walking the thin line between loving son and *Yes, I know my mom's nuts.*

"Hi," she said, the Realtor smile never slipping.

I needed to say something fast before Mom started telling Dakota stories about my potty training. But all of Miss Apricots's fakeness made it hard to focus.

"Do you know my mom from the"—*Don't say death*—"uh…the restaurant?"

"No, we go way back."

I raised an eyebrow.

Her smile grew an impossible millimeter wider. "I manage the house your family's renting. So I've spoken to Gladys over the phone, emailed, texted, given her house keys, so…"

"BFFs."

She gave a fake laugh. "Pretty much."

"Hopefully, the matching bracelets are engraved in time."

"Fingers crossed."

There was a pause that promised to turn awkward. Mom and Casey were busy fine-tuning tomorrow's schedule, but Mom had sonar for when she should swoop. Which left me blurting out the first thing that came to mind. "When the guy died, why did the waitress say, *Not again*?"

Immediately, Dakota's demeanor changed. Her smile grew harder, and her eyes went steely. Maybe Mom should have talked about how I used to pull off my diaper and streak around the house.

"Sorry. You knew him." I ran a hand through my hair. "That was rude."

"It's fine. Like Bea said, it wasn't the first time."

"That he's had an episode?"

"No," She shifted to check the pickup counter. She sighed when her order wasn't ready. "It wasn't the first time I came across a dead body."

I didn't know what to say to that.

Fiddling with an earring, she went on. "You could say I've had a string of bad luck the past couple of years."

"Ohh-kay..." That was super vague. I tried again. "Was it checking a rental?"

"Once." Dakota began tugging at the earring. "You heard about DJ Hughes's murder?"

"DJ Hughes? That was here?" My voice rose, and Mom glanced over. DJ Hughes had been a staple on America's Top 40. Then, on vacation, he'd been found murdered at the bottom of a grand staircase. Lowering my voice, I asked, "That was you?"

"Yeah. I found him while checking the property."

"At our rental?"

She laughed, actually laughed—not like her fake smiles. "No. He rented the Caldwell Mansion overlooking the cove."

I wasn't a huge fan of his music, but I got sucked into the sensationalized media coverage. They caught the killer pretty quickly, and then there were plenty of courtroom clips during the trial. I could picture the guy's face but not his name.

"The publicist did it?" I asked.

"His manager pushed him down the grand staircase."

I shuddered. "That'd be freaky. And you kept managing rentals after finding him?"

"I mean, yeah. It's a family thing, and it was sort of my turn. Besides"—she sat up a little taller—"I haven't found other bodies in the rentals."

"Still, *death in the diner* could bring up some unpleasant memories."

"Well..." She pulled out her earring and looked at it. "There's been more."

"More what?"

"Dakota, your order's ready," a voice yelled from the counter. She stood and beamed at my mother. "Thanks for the seat."

I expected her to leave without answering, but then she looked me straight in the eye and said, "There have been more bodies."

# CHAPTER 4

Dakota was gone before I could ask how many bodies. Somehow I managed a conversation with Nigel about diversified portfolios when I really wanted to pull out my phone and search for headlines and obituaries in Amelia's Haven. My headache had dulled, but talking about compounding interest was rekindling the flames. You can't choose your family, and you definitely can't choose their spouses.

Harper was on Nigel's lap. Juniper was leaning against Jude. Mom and Casey were still talking, while Dad was helping Baxter draw. The first full day of our *Awesome Vacay* was winding down, and my parents hadn't announced any life-shattering revelations. Could the dead guy or my afternoon nap have thrown a wrench in their schedule? I shouldn't have been disappointed. Actually, instead of being disappointed, I was annoyed. If nothing was wrong, then Mom got me to come to this gross beach town under false pretenses.

The meal's check hadn't been paid when Mom instructed Dad and me to go to the van ahead of the circus to get the car started. I was fading fast and in danger of saying something incredibly offensive out loud—rude thoughts kept on the inside don't count. Also, Dad had been around people all day and needed some quiet.

Mom and Dad had driven to Amelia's Haven in Dad's Corvette right after grading finals. When Dad picked me up at the Carentorrie Airport he'd been driving the Corvette. If he'd warned me about the family fun bus waiting at the rental house, the desire to take the next flight home might have overpowered any family obligations.

The relationship I had with my father was built on a foundation of silence and was one of my best relationships. If there was trouble in my parents' lives, I wouldn't hear about it from him. But at least he was someone I could be quiet around.

My favorite memory was when Dad and I bailed on my mom and sisters at Disney World after too many days of chaos masquerading as fun. We stayed in our hotel room, napped, watched TV, and read before getting pizza and going to bed early. They say Disney World is the happiest place on earth. In my opinion, escaping the crowds, noise, and heat made our hotel room the happiest place.

Five minutes alone in the van wasn't the same as that whole day of freedom, but it was way better than spending one more second at our crowded table.

It had begun drizzling during supper, so we jogged to the van. Once inside, Dad turned on the windshield wipers, and we were safe from the rain and family. I began rubbing my temples while Dad pulled out a book. Dad's reading was a staple in life and was strangely soothing. Paperback books would always appear around him since he hated e-readers.

"What's that?" I asked.

"*The Maltese Falcon*," he said. "A 1930s detective novel."

Had he chosen a crime novel before a man dropped dead? I didn't want to know. So, instead, I asked the question I was dreading the answer to. "Anything else scheduled tonight?"

Dad sighed. "No."

With that, I could truly relax. My garage oasis was waiting. I could hide out and watch a movie on my laptop. Now I wanted my family to pile into the van. The sooner they arrived, the sooner my social engagements would be over.

Nigel and Casey were the first to appear, each of them carrying a kid.

Where could Dad go in a house full of people? He had his book, but would that be enough? The man had nowhere to hide. "I'm gonna watch a movie in the garage. You're welcome to join."

Dad let out a breath, his relief obvious. "I'll bring the beer."

The drive back to the rental was surprisingly painless. I was evacuating from the van before Dad had it in park, giving Mom no chance to suggest a board game. After walking up the garage's plywood staircase, I evaluated my room for the next five nights. My suitcase was organized, and the foldout bed was banished. The only thing out of place was the mint shirt I'd tossed on the floor. I didn't love the space, but at least there was privacy.

With Dad expected any minute, I took my wrinkled vacay shirt from the floor and hung it in the shower. Dad came with a couple of beers and sat in the armchair while I took the couch. I put on *Die Hard*.

*Die Hard*'s technically a Christmas movie, but I'm a warm and fuzzy guy who can watch Christmas movies (if they're *Die Hard*) year-round.

We both let out a long sigh as we settled in to watch.

Gruber was entering Nakatomi Plaza when Juniper and Jude entered my lair. They must have understood the rule of silence because they made their way to the couch and slid in. Juniper sat in the middle, holding Jude's hand but resting her head on my shoulder. "I missed you," she murmured.

"Yeah," I said, shifting to get more comfortable.

The laptop on the sea chest was one thing when it was Dad and me. But it wasn't ideal for mass viewing. Was Juniper resting her head on my shoulder so she could see? Could Jude even see the screen?

John McClane had just clipped Heinrich when Casey made an appearance. I know I'm a jerk, but I really didn't want to pause the movie and squish a fourth adult onto the couch. Only to have her start complaining when she couldn't see. Thankfully, she sat on the floor by my armrest and leaned her head on my knee.

"The kids are down," she said, with the crazed look parents get.

"Mom?" Juniper asked.

"Cleaning something."

"Nigel?" Now I was doing it.

"His allergies flared from the potted plants at The Marina. He took a Benadryl and went to bed."

With that, we all sat watching John McClane do what only John McClane could. Maybe my family wasn't so bad.

We were nearly to the bloody kiss in the back of the limo when Mom appeared in the doorway. She watched us instead of the movie and took photos when she thought we weren't looking.

When the credits started, she came and sat on Dad's armrest, stretching her legs across him. She took his hand. Was it time for the announcement?

*Well, kids, we've been keeping this a secret for too long…*

I sat up a little.

"Casey and I couldn't decide on mini golf and then brunch or breakfast, then mini golf."

With that, the beautiful companionable silence was shattered. I was once again about to have a meltdown from too much family time. The problem was everyone was hanging out in my bedroom. Short of leaving to crash on the living room couch and risk waking up to Baxter using my stomach as a trampoline, I was trapped.

"Would we eat at the same place regardless?" Juniper asked, lifting her head from my shoulder.

I tried not to groan. This could take all night.

Years of experience had taught me that my vote wouldn't count. It was easier not to fight the tide and allow it to drag me under.

I crossed my arms, leaned back, and closed my eyes.

"Good night, champ," Dad said, patting my shoulder before making his exit—with Jude a couple of steps behind. Unfortunately, no one else took the hint. Mom took Dad's seat, and Casey took Jude's.

*Mini Golf v. Brunch* would begin with opening arguments.

I'm becoming an old man. My whole plan to pretend to sleep so everyone leaves backfired when I actually fell asleep.

Somehow I tipped over from my reclined position and woke up hours later to a face full of drool and leather. My gaping mouth was right where Jude's butt had been. His board shorts had spent an entire day sitting on dirt, diner booths, and bird poo.

The room was dark, my computer was shut, and I was covered in a blanket. I'd had a weird dream where Dakota and Mr. FunRun were riding seahorses at each other like they were jousting. Was that supposed to mean something?

Checking the time, my phone read 4:47 a.m. That's what sleeping half the day got me. Why couldn't today be the sunrise hike? Under normal circumstances, I would have fallen back asleep, yet when I closed my eyes, I saw seahorses.

Awake but not alert, I took a shower—trying not to bang my elbows along the sides. Coffee would have to wait until someone was awake in the big house to let me in. Yesterday's events began playing through my semi-rested brain. I can't be considered smart without at least two cups of coffee, but the dead guy next to a seahorse mural had definitely happened. If Dakota had made up Amelia's Haven being the site of DJ Hughes's murder, the internet would quickly set me to rights. But wasn't there something else in that never-ending fever dream of a day? Hadn't Miss Apricots said *bodies*?

Maybe the reason for the fantastic group rate Mom got was because the whole place was a massive death trap. There was something wrong with this place beyond the obvious ocean, sand, and way too many tourists. I'd been right to hate this place.

Opening my computer, I created a file and typed up the details I remembered. What had Dakota meant when she said "more bodies"? Were they murders, or did she double as a hospice worker?

With that, I launched my official Amelia's Haven murder search. DJ Hughes was the easiest to fact-check. Hundreds of results popped up from DJ Hughes's murder. I remembered the basics from the passing interest I'd taken. However, rereading the articles took on a new life, being in the town and knowing the rental agent.

Dakota's story was quickly confirmed. The murder happened at the Caldwell Mansion in Amelia's Haven, Oregon. Skimming the articles, I tried to find an image or reference to Miss Apricots. Easier said than done.

Do you have any idea how many tribute videos were made for DJ Hughes? People remixing his remixes—most of them excruciatingly painful.

For the longest time, all I got was the line *This renowned artist was found dead by the property manager.* Then I found it. A photo of Miss Apricots in the middle of a musical montage of different pictures of the case. Pausing at the pic, I took it all in. The photo was slightly out of focus. Dakota was handcuffed, gazing at my detective friend from the diner. Instead of looking mad or guilty, she was excited. There were lots of captions at the bottom of the image, saying stuff like:

#DJHughes

#murderer?

#localgirl

#abunchofothercrapididntbotherreading.

Deep diving into the comments, I hoped to find more info on the shot of Dakota. That was asking a lot. This video was nothing like a college paper, where you had to cite your sources.

I jumped when there was a knock at my door.

"Hello?" I said, making my voice deep to intimidate potential murderers.

Juniper's laugh came through the door. "Are you decent?"

"Yeah."

Juniper popped her head in. She was wearing spandex leggings with her social media logo on the calf. Did fans actually buy those?

"Do you want to join Jude and me for sunrise yoga?"

"Uh…"

"Optional event on the itinerary. Locals go, but it's open for tourists too."

I didn't answer.

She popped her hip. "You're already up, and it's on the beach as the sun rises. It's a once-in-a-lifetime opportunity."

"That all your followers will get to share in?"

"If I have a glorious experience on the beach, they all get to share in it."

She'd said sunrise. So far the Oregon Coast was behaving pretty similarly to Seattle. "Isn't it raining?"

Juniper hesitated for half a second. "That was last night."

"Is it cloudy?"

"Well…"

I frowned. "Is rain likely? And it's by the ocean, so it'll be windy. Also, we won't see the sunrise. Do you know what the tide's doing?"

"Please?" She made a little-sister face. "I covered your mother-child bonding spot yesterday so you could get some beauty sleep."

"Yoga as payback for a stay of execution?"

Juniper grinned. "It's a start. You'll still owe me." She came closer, and I closed my laptop, hiding my murder board. Arching a brow, she said, "Unless you're too busy."

She wanted me to go. And I didn't want to explain why I was cyberstalking DJ Hughes. Which would come up if I declined.

"If there's coffee in the van, I can be down in five."

"Perfect."

Once the door closed, I took a screenshot of Dakota in handcuffs.

# CHAPTER 5

Yoga with Juniper was today's first attempt to embrace a better attitude. Easy, breezy, go-with-the-flow, or whatever the beachside instructor was suggesting. I was nowhere near zenning out. But that also meant I wasn't about to fall asleep meditating—which happened the last time Juniper made me do yoga.

The early-morning chill had most of the yogis in long sleeves and hats. A few rays from the sun broke through the cloud cover, but overall the day threatened rain. Wind picked up bits of sand, which pelted us through the postures. It was quite unpleasant.

I don't know what's with the obsession with sunrise in Amelia's Haven. Statistically, it's a fifty-fifty shot of being overcast. And why would people on the West Coast participate in sunrise yoga? Maybe sunset yoga, if watching the sun falling into the ocean's your thing. But sunrise? Amelia's Haven is weird.

There was a woman, one yoga mat down and two over, who caught my eye. The weather didn't bother her. She had rich black hair pulled back in a ponytail and wore a rose-colored tank showing off her biceps. Sure she was attractive. But believe it or not, plenty of attractive women were doing seaside yoga. I knew her…didn't I?

But I didn't know anyone in Amelia's Haven. I ran through my list of acquaintances. She wasn't a coworker. Maybe a college class? Or had we shared a ski lift?

After our final namaste, I was rolling up the mat I'd had to buy at a ridiculous markup when our eyes met. Then it hit me. She was my EMT or paramedic…not sure what the difference is. She saw the moment recognition hit. Her eyes danced as the color drained from my face.

I hadn't been at my best yesterday. Still, I should have recognized her profile when I saw it during Warrior One. This version of her wasn't wearing a uniform or latex gloves. Even so, she was unforgettable.

Of course, I didn't say anything. Instead, I stared at her like I'd never seen a woman before.

She gave a quick nod. "Glad to see you've recovered."

What should I say? My options were laughing it off, groaning, or insulting her. I settled on the perfect answer. "Uh…" She started to leave, but I needed to clear the air after the burping-in-her-face incident. "Sorry!" I blurted. She turned back. "Sorry and thank you. I'm hazy on some of the details, but I remember you were excellent." I cracked a smile. "Not many people can get my mother to change her mind."

A touch of color hit her cheeks, and she bobbed her head. "My pleasure."

Silence. Again.

Running a hand through my hair, I tried to think of something to say.

"Well," she said, "for me, it was part of the job, but there's no way you were prepared for a lunchtime emergency." Our eyes met. "From what I heard, you were the only one who tried to help."

"Oh, uh…" Was I blushing? "I was a lifeguard in college. Guess it stuck."

A smile played on her lips. "You almost sound like a good person."

"I did it for the bikinis."

"Creeper."

I grinned. "Believe it or not, I've been called worse."

Her lips quirked as she tried not to laugh. "Oh, I believe it."

Something in her tone brought back the phone conversation I'd overheard in the ambulance. Had she been notifying someone about the death?

"Did you know him?" I asked.

When she frowned, there was the ghost of a scar beside her right eyebrow. "We got to know each other. He was in the area for a few months."

I nodded. Attempting to be sympathetic—or empathetic?

"We shared a similar problem. He was helping me," she said. "With him gone, I'll need to start over."

What problem? And what was the deal with Mr. FunRun? What tied him to my EMT and Miss Apricots? Both women were half his age, or even younger. I get it's a small town, but how had they met, let alone shared problems?

Without thinking, I said, "Let me know if I can help." Why would I say that? And why did I want her to accept the offer?

Her eyes lingered on my face, analyzing me before she answered. "Thanks. It's been an unusual couple of years." She shook her head. "Still, I didn't expect someone to poison Allen's sweet tea."

I nodded. "Yeah."

Then I replayed her last sentence. She'd said poison. The sweet tea was poisoned. The sweet tea I'd almost knocked over was poisoned? I'd almost spilled a cup of poison?

The sand beneath me shifted. Suddenly hands were gripping my elbow, steadying me.

"Sorry," she said. "You didn't know. It's all over town. But maybe just with the locals." This was the second person to make a cryptic comment about the death rate in Amelia's Haven. What was up with this place?

Then, realizing she still held my elbow, I shrugged and said, "I'm fine. It's fine."

She let go of my arm. Giving a nervous laugh, she tucked invisible strands of hair behind her ear. A large diamond glittered on her ring finger. Was she married? Obviously I didn't care. This was just a visit.

Jude and Juniper were waiting by our tour bus, yoga mats in hand. It was time to go. To pry further into the poisoning, I'd need at least a second (or third) cup of coffee.

"Well, thanks," I said before it got more awkward. Then I remembered a question I really needed to ask. "Sorry if you said and I forgot...but what's your name?"

Her eyes sparkled. "It's Asato. Brittany Asato."

I was no longer the only one to introduce myself like James Bond. Grinning, I said, "Bye, Brittany."

"Bye, Holt."

When I got to the van, Jude was in the driver's seat, but Juniper waited on the sand, ready to pounce. "Do you know who you were talking to?" she asked.

"Her name's Brittany."

Juniper blinked. "Impressive. What else do you know about her?"

"Beyond her job, not much." Her being married didn't matter. Opening the door for shotgun, when Juniper didn't move, I took the front seat and hoped the topic would be dropped.

Juniper climbed into the back, and Jude began to drive. "Well, I started talking with Agnes and Loretta after class and—"

"Who?"

"Agnes and Loretta."

That cleared it up.

"Agnes had the white pixie cut, and Loretta had the blondish hair—technically a wig, but don't tell anyone."

"And you know these people?"

"Like I said, we started talking after class. They saw Brittany with a strange man, and then I said you were my brother, and then they said her fiancé was murdered and her twin brother was arrested for the crime!"

"What?"

"It gets even spookier. The fiancé was one of the beachside yoga instructors and was found before class, lying in Corpse Pose, stabbed to death."

My temples began flaming. I definitely needed more coffee. "Juniper, you can't believe everything people tell you. Annie and Lauren decided to tease a gullible tourist."

"Holt."

I met her eyes.

"Trust me. They were telling the truth."

Trust Juniper? She did have a way with people. It was annoying.

Shrugging, I was glad when Juniper didn't push. If the murdered fiancé story was true, my official thoughts were: Terrible news. So awful for everyone involved.

Off the record, I was left with one critical question: Was Brittany single?

---

The ever-present itinerary was successfully updated last night after I fell asleep. With the return of the yogis, the whole family would set off for mini golf. This was the perfect plan, taking every possible factor into account…except for the fact that Casey had two toddlers.

Three tantrums and one meltdown later (none of them mine), last night's expertly laid mini-golf plans were set aside for brunch—a brunch that was getting closer and closer to lunch.

On the drive over, Baxter dumped his orange juice on me, then cried about the spilled juice while I had to sit in a sticky pair of designer shorts. Prior to this visit, it had been years since I'd worn coffee or juice on my clothes. What can I say? Kids are great.

We ended up at a Victorian B and B. The house was cool enough on the outside, but the inside was full of glass dolls with painted eyes. First seahorses, now dolls? What was with this town having creepy-eyed things stare down at you? Was being constantly watched inciting homicidal rage? If that was the problem, the town could be fixed with a few renovations and some dump runs.

*Don't make eye contact with the haunted dolls. Be at peace. Smile…smile…don't grimace.*

I really tried, sitting there in my sticky shorts without complaint. We ordered our food, and I got more coffee. But there was so much going on. Baxter was on Casey's lap, snuffling about his lost juice. Jude and Juniper were whispering and making googly eyes at each other. Mom declaring we'd play a game of Would You Rather was one thing too many. I excused myself and escaped to the back deck.

It had warmed up since yoga, but the day remained overcast. I was comfortable in my shorts and pullover with sunglasses. Sliding into an Adirondack, I waited for the ringing to leave my ears. If I was normal, the ocean view and crashing waves would have been soothing or majestic. But since it's me, I was more inclined to be agoraphobic.

Pulling out my phone, I began scrolling aimlessly through social media. Then I remembered Juniper had interrupted me before I could do my due diligence on Dakota's other bodies. My new search started with the *death of a yogi* Juniper had mentioned. I was disappointed by the utter lack of info. Amelia's Haven didn't have a proper news outlet. The town was too small to bother. Broadening the search to *Amelia's Haven murder*, I was back to all the repetitive articles on DJ Hughes.

I needed a new plan.

Typing *Amelia's Haven obituaries* didn't prove immediately helpful. But at least DJ Hughes's face wasn't plastered everywhere. It would help if I knew people's names. I'd heard Mr. FunRun's name. Something like Aaron or Eric, but I couldn't quite remember.

I sighed. My family would know Mr. FunRun's name. Juniper would usually be my first choice, but yoga had left her amorous, and she wouldn't check her phone. Dad wouldn't know. If I texted Mom, she might ask me to come inside. Which left Casey.

I texted: *What's the dead diner guy's name?*

Within seconds she replied: *Allen Fisher.*

I remembered to say thanks before taking off with my new lead. *Allen Fisher* generated thousands of results, most notably for a boxer and a poet. Trying *Allen Fisher Amelia's Haven* didn't help. Then, remembering our Rainy Days 10K shirts, I tried adding *Seattle* after his name.

It took a bit of scrolling, but Allen's face finally popped up. There was an old bio of him working as a photographer for a nature magazine. At the bottom, the bio was updated to say, *Congrats to Allen, who in retirement is fulfilling his dream of full-time birdwatching.*

Birdwatching? He was a total nerd.

Brittany had said Allen was helping her with a problem. She wasn't into birdwatching...right?

Since his name combined with Amelia's Haven had already proved useless, I got creative. I reinstalled my Facebook app, then reset the password. Next, I tried to find a page for Amelia's Haven birdwatchers. It was a real low point in my life. Instead of birdwatching, I found the town's weekly bingo page and a group dedicated to the best places to watch the moon.

Allen was retired. My head snapped up. Retirement? Was that why Mom and Dad had gathered us? Were they announcing their exit from the rat race for the golden years? If correct, it'd be a tad melodramatic.

Could they afford retirement? How much did two college professors make? On the one hand, Dad had a Corvette. On the other, was it paid off? This also begged the question, how old were my parents? I had no clue. Juniper would be no help, saying, "Uh, Dad's older." Casey would know, but then she'd know I didn't know...I wanted to say midfifties, but if they were pushing seventy, would I know the difference?

Another text came in from Casey: *You good?*

You'd think she was my big sister instead of two years younger. Was she worried I was racked with grief about Mr. FunRun—I mean Allen?

I sent the classy thumbs-up emoji.

Casey: *Sorry again about Baxter. Nigel thinks he should be enrolled in martial arts for better hand-eye coordination...lol.*

Me: *I'm scared for my life.*

Dots started to process on her side before disappearing.

Finally, I sent: *Can you let me know when the food's ready?*

It was Casey's turn to send a thumbs-up.

During our exchange, a couple of employees had snuck onto the deck and were taking a breather. Slouched as I was in an Adirondack, they didn't see me.

Someone began speaking. The voice could belong to no other than a teenage girl sharing a secret. "...this time, it was poison."

Obviously, I was intrigued. More dirt on Mr. FunRun...or Allen. Still, how many reminders did a guy need to never eat again?

A male voice began. By the way it cracked, another teen. "Yeah, poison makes more sense. That last one—the trident stabbing at the aquarium fundraiser—was weird. Who chooses a trident?"

Peeking behind me, I saw that the B and B waitress looked like the waitress at The Dining Seahorse, who'd said, *Not again!*

She continued. "Detective Reynolds questioned me because I was at the register when it happened. He wanted to know if Ms. Persephone got me to do it because of a restaurant rivalry."

"You were actually questioned by Detective Reynolds?" The boy's voice squeaked.

"Yeah. When he wasn't accusing me of murder, he was asking for copies from the register's camera and the bills of people who paid in the ten to twenty minutes before Allen died."

"Well, it's finally your turn," the guy said.

"I know! Took long enough," she said. "Carlos thinks—"

"Carlos? Why talk to Carlos?"

"All I meant was—"

"If Carlos knew anything, he'd leave you alone," the kid grumbled.

The girl's voice turned teasing. "I'll tell him the next time I see him."

"Next time? Like guitar playing at midnight is better than surfing with me?"

The giggle changed to an attempt at seduction. "I'll never tell."

During their exchange, Casey had texted, saying the food was ready. Besides, I'd quickly lost interest when their discussion shifted from murders to *The Bachelorette*. There was a reason I liked being single.

When I stood, you'd think I was a corpse rising from the grave, the way they screamed and clung to each other.

"Morning," I said. Then added, "Give Carlos my best."

# **CHAPTER 6**

Halfway through brunch, mini golf was officially canceled. I don't know why Mom bothers with meticulous planning. Even when nobody drops dead in diners, there are so many variables that Mom spends her family vacations with tension headaches.

What couldn't be postponed for a second day was my appointment for mother-child bonding.

Dad never scheduled alone time with his children. He went along with a lot of Mom's stuff, but even he had his limits. He always said, "I don't need an appointment to hang out with my kids." And he didn't. Somehow or another, Dad would always be around for special moments. It was Mom who needed them scheduled.

When I met Mom in the driveway, she tossed me the keys to Dad's Corvette. "Do you mind driving us into town?"

"Sure," I said, unable to hide my grin.

The trip from our rental to Amelia's Haven's business district was around a mile. Though how any town could consider one street with a few blocks of stores an actual business district is beyond me. At any rate, I was always willing to drive Dad's baby, no matter the distance.

Mom directed me toward a city parking lot. "Since you had to rest yesterday, I went rock climbing with Juniper. So now you're on Juniper's date."

She looked at me expectantly. Did she want me to apologize for the inconvenience?

"What?"

"In the schedule, I left it open to start with the ice cream and end with a stroll or vice versa."

How would I know that?

"Um, let's walk."

We made it three steps before Mom stopped. There was a display on the sidewalk full of postcards showing tons of sites for Amelia's Haven and the surrounding area. A sign boasted a thousand more options inside.

Mom frowned and checked the time.

"Do you want to buy some postcards?" I asked.

"Well, since we're here, it would be convenient to find postcards for the ladies in book group. But I don't want to take away from our time together."

"Might as well get them while we're here."

"Are you sure?"

I smiled. "Take all the time you need."

The shop's door was half-open when she asked, "Do you want to help me choose?"

I shook my head. There was no way I was going into the store with her. I refused to be dragged into questions about whether Mrs. Palmer would prefer the sunset by the lighthouse or the full moon at the pier.

Sitting on a city bench, I waited, peacefully scrolling through my phone. This was an unexpected reprieve…or so I thought.

I sensed the obnoxious presence before I saw him. The town's detective didn't actually smell like sweat or rotten onions, but he should have. Would Juniper say his aura needed cleansing?

Looking up, I found my detective friend standing a little too close. He didn't say anything. He was too busy staring down at me. Probably an intimidation tactic he learned on YouTube.

Putting my phone away, I tried to be folksy. "Afternoon," I said.

"Mr. Jacobs, I have some follow-up questions."

It was tempting to tell the cop any questions had to go through my attorney for no other reason than to watch his face turn red. But I controlled myself—Mom would be proud.

"All right." I nodded toward the bench, but the officer remained standing. The guy was short, but that didn't mean I was nuts about him hovering over me.

"Why were you contaminating an active crime scene?" he asked.

Excuse me?

I frowned. "I don't know what you're talking about."

The detective took a step closer, and I had the childish desire to crawl over the bench to put some space between us. "Allen was dead when he hit the floor. Why would you try to save a dead man unless you'd killed him and were giving yourself a reason to have your DNA all over the body?"

I should have gone the lawyer route...

Deciding not to back down, I stood up and towered over the detective. "I performed first aid. There were no ulterior motives." Maybe I should've stopped there. But I kept talking. "CPR is literally designed for when someone's heart stops."

My cop friend's eyes dilated. "I saw you on the security camera. You bumped into Allen during the time frame he was poisoned."

"Everyone knows I was at the restaurant." I took a step closer—if he didn't care about personal space, neither did I. "But if I remember correctly, you were at the register during that same time frame. Is anyone questioning you?"

That may have been too far. The cop's face turned so red, I wondered if he'd need first aid. His mouth opened and closed, but no words came out.

"Is there anything else, Officer?"

"Detective," he managed.

"Right." I gave my least condescending smile. "Anything else?"

"Not right now," he barked and strode away.

He had to save face somehow. I was tempted to applaud but restrained myself.

As I went to sit back down, I was stopped by Mom exiting the boutique, carrying a brown bag full of postcards.

"Ready?" she asked.

I watched the detective turn down a street before nodding. "Ready."

The town was relatively quiet. Most of the tourists were by the ocean, ignoring the wind and clouds. Neither one of us spoke as we passed the first few buildings. She crooked her arm in mine like it was prom or she was an old lady—which is weirder?

Instead of enjoying the waves or whatever beachy stuff people are into, I was stuck worrying about what topics Mom would choose to discuss. I didn't have long to wait.

These scheduled bonding times weren't my thing. Mom would start out really quiet, hoping I'd open up, and if I didn't, she'd go full interrogation. The problem was I didn't have anything to open up about. No recent girlfriends, and work was fine.

We'd walked about a block in silence before Mom decided to take control. "You know I worry about you."

I groaned. "Why? I'm debt-free, have a good job, a nice place, enjoy cooking, eat a decent amount of vegetables, and work out."

"You do."

She'd given me that point, yet I knew there was a *but* coming.

"You've created a nice-looking life," she continued. "But aren't you lonely?"

There it was. Since we'd been having versions of this conversation for years, I was ready.

"Mom, I'm not going to date the daughter of one of your college friends. I did that once, which was once too many."

"Holt, that was six years ago. And I've explained many times that I'd heard nothing but great things about Marguerite. No one said she was an amateur taxidermist!"

I shuddered. "Don't know why since that's all she talked about."

"Well, if you ever change your mind, Marguerite has a sister who collects milk bottles."

"Milk bottles? Let's set it up."

Mom swatted my shoulder.

In the following silence, I came up with a safe conversation topic. "It's been cool seeing everyone without the added stress of Christmas or a wedding getting mixed in."

I left out the part about being stressed guessing what was so wrong with her or Dad that she felt the need to summon us all. This wasn't counter-reconnaissance. All I needed was her nose out of my business.

The nostalgia did the trick. Soon enough, Mom was talking about Juniper's wedding and the bridesmaid who ordered a dress two sizes too small and didn't bother trying it on before the big day. Mom even got a couple of laughs out of me.

The walk being a smashing success, we made our way to Amelia's Creamery, boasting eighteen artisan flavors of ice cream. Mom chose Summer Haze, which was an ice cream flavored with honey and lavender. I went for something less gross with an equally ridiculous name. Sandy Shore was vanilla ice cream with caramel swirls and bits of chocolate.

Mom paid the older cashier while I held her waffle cone and waited for another teenage girl to finish scooping mine. On the wall behind her was a photo of a woman with graying hair laughing by a hummingbird. There was a black ribbon tied across the picture frame.

"Her name was Lizzy," said the teen in a baby doll voice.

I was so surprised by the toddler's voice coming from a teen's body, I didn't comprehend what she said. "Hm?"

"The picture."

"Right." I nodded. And since my sleuthing senses were tingling, I added, "I can't remember the symbolism of the different colored ribbons. What's the black ribbon mean?"

"Death." Her voice was so childish, I fought the urge to laugh.

"Oh, I'm sorry," I said, almost behaving like an adult.

The girl shrugged. "I didn't know her." Handing me my cone, she glanced at the man at the register. "She was murdered by her boyfriend. They were both birdwatchers. He took his binoculars and—"

"Katie!" the man yelled.

Katie gave him me a sugary smile and handed over the cone. "Enjoy."

The man also tried to smile, but it was forced. As we left, he began whispering to the teen, "Tourists don't come here to hear about murders. You can't keep—" He shut up fast when he realized I was still in the shop. Mom had gone outside, and I could only linger by the napkins for so long.

I pretended I hadn't been eavesdropping and left the shop with way too many napkins.

Mom had chosen a spot on the patio by a massive display of hanging flowers. She was enjoying her first taste of Summer Haze, but I hesitated.

"Did a bug fly in your ice cream?" Mom asked.

"No, it's..." How do you tell your mom her cozy vacation spot was murder central? "Does anything seem off to you about this town?"

She lowered her waffle cone. "Yes, I know the beach wouldn't be your first choice, but the location in relation to where everyone lived made it the best option."

Reminding myself I was an adult, not a teenager, I did my best to answer calmly. "I have kept my complaining to an absolute minimum!"

"While turning your eye-rolling to the absolute maximum?"

This is why I keep silent. It all gets screwed up if I talk. Taking a deep breath, I tried again. "Sorry, that came out wrong. Um…well…DJ Hughes was murdered here."

"The one who did 'Put Some Sugar on It'?"

I choked on a bite of waffle cone. Mom knew that song?

After a bout of coughing, I said, "That's him."

Mom weighed her options before speaking. "So, finding out a music artist was murdered here after that man had a heart attack is upsetting you?"

"What? No." I ran a hand through my hair. "There were more deaths."

"Okay." Mom was teetering between frustrated and sympathetic. The tone she chose was an attempt at placating. "You realize people die all the time?"

I opened my mouth and shut it again. Suddenly a little kid, unable to speak up.

"Holt, I'm sorry that poor man had a heart attack and died. Still, there's no need for conspiracy theories on how this whole town is haunted."

"I never said haunted" was my stellar comeback.

Did I bring up how Allen died from poisoning instead of a heart attack? Mention the murdered birdwatcher or the yoga killer? No, I didn't. Why would I give details to support my case when fighting with my mother?

We finished our ice cream in silence before returning to the house. I went up to my room to decompress during my budgeted quiet time while Mom probably used hers to tell Dad how sulky I was.

# CHAPTER 7

After taking a shower, I put on a workout shirt. I'd be layering up for anything else Mom had planned, and it was nice to be casual during the scheduled break. I pulled up my Amelia's Haven murder file and was adding in the new info when someone began climbing the stairs.

"Knock-knock," they called.

Too annoying for anyone in my family. Also, my family knew *quiet time* translated to *Leave Holt alone or he's not responsible for his actions.*

"It's open," I called, closing my laptop.

Miss Apricots—or Dakota—walked in with a disposable coffee cup. "Hi, Holt." She beamed. Today, instead of an apricot dress, she wore a red shirt with a skirt covered with cherries. Just like yesterday, the look was a bit much.

"Hey," I said.

She didn't say anything else.

Was she waiting for me to do something? I don't know what she expected. Dakota was the one who barged in on me.

Finally, she took a step forward. "I brought you some hot cocoa," she said, extending the cup with a Willows' Rentals sticker along the side.

I blinked. While the day wasn't hot, the month was still May. It wasn't December. We weren't attending a winter parade. And was she really calling it hot *cocoa*? What's wrong with regular old hot chocolate? And who brings hot chocolate to an adult? At least make it a mocha, so there's some caffeine.

"Thanks," I managed, taking the cup.

That was all the invitation she needed. Next thing I knew, she was settling into the armchair.

"Did you know Allen?" she asked.

"Who?"

So I played a little dumb. At least I'm not the one barging in on men during their scheduled quiet times.

I'd confused her.

"Um." She pursed her lips. "Allen Fisher…the dead guy."

"Oh, right." I frowned like his name was new information. "I didn't know him. Why would I?"

"Your shirt. It's the same one Allen was wearing."

Huh. I was indeed wearing my Rainy Days 10K shirt.

I'd had the good fortune to not only pack but subconsciously wear a shirt that linked me to a murder victim. I don't even do fun runs. It was a date with a girl I met at the gym, and the relationship didn't make it through the race. I don't remember her name, and the only reason I know the fun run's name is because Rainy Days 10K was on the stupid shirt.

Still, I didn't need to explain myself to my mother's rental agent. I stood. "So, Seattle's a city. There were quite a few people at the race. I didn't meet everyone."

She remained seated, unbothered by my cold reception. "Right, well, I'm so sorry you were at the restaurant when it happened."

"Thanks." What would it take for her to leave?

She started to shift forward, teasing me with the thought she was leaving. Instead, she said, "After what happened, I tossed and turned all night."

"Okay."

Dakota's eyes widened unnaturally, like she was expecting me to say more. But since I'm a grown-up who doesn't like weird small talk with strangers, I kept silent.

Hold on. Why exactly had she stopped by with a cup of cocoa? I replayed her questions and meaningful looks. Was she trying to interrogate me?

"Had you seen him around town?" she tried.

So, yeah. She was definitely milking me for information. Little did she realize what living eighteen years with Mom had trained me for.

Wait. I was trapped in a room with the town's busybody. She was the one who dealt with multiple *bodies.* She knew everything about this death trap. As intrusive as her little drop-in was, I could use it to my advantage. All I needed to do was ask the right questions.

"I only saw him at the diner." Then, not wanting to show my hand, I tried a roundabout approach. "Did his job keep him active in the community?"

"Not exactly. He was retired." Dakota sat there, perfectly unaware of the turning tides.

"But you knew him?" I took a sip of the overly sweet hot chocolate and managed not to gag.

"Kind of. He came here as a tourist and decided to stay a few months."

She was taking the bait. Now to reel her in gently. "Why's that?"

"He was visiting with a group of birdwatchers. There was an accident. Well, technically a murder, and Allen stayed after the case was closed. The killer got away. Allen had been close friends with him. I think Allen hoped if he stayed, he'd be able to find his friend and get him to turn himself in."

I was preparing my next question when a surprised look crossed Dakota's face, and she stood.

Not so fun being interrogated.

As much as I wanted her gone, there was still so much I didn't know about this horrible town. "So Allen was investigating?" I kept my face blank as she scanned me suspiciously. Would she bother answering or just leave?

"I guess," she said. "He'd go birdwatching in the mornings, then spend his afternoons talking to locals."

"He kept busy."

"Busier than some people." Dakota gave an awkward laugh. I'd really knocked her off her game. As she moved, I noticed a cherry necklace that matched her skirt. "Well, thank you for your time," she said. "I had to come by to check the grill and thought I'd better see how you were holding up." She gave me one of her award-winning Realtor smiles.

I nodded. "Drive safe." And gave an equally fake smile.

The door didn't hit her on the way out, but it's a good thing she didn't dawdle.

Returning to my laptop, I checked my murder file's progress. The little I knew of Brittany's yoga fiancé's death and the trident aquarium murder was in the file. I was beginning to add in the details I'd learned about the birdwatching murder, when my phone buzzed.

Mom had messaged the family group text: *It's time for EVERYONE to come to the big house for the next family outing.*

She could have just said: *Holt, you're late.*

Dakota had stolen my quiet time. And all I'd gotten was a cup of overly sweet hot cocoa.

Rubbing my face in my hands, I tried to prepare myself for another evening of family fun. If I didn't appear soon, someone would come get me. After dumping the rest of the cocoa down the bathroom sink, I grabbed a pullover and left my garage hideaway.

When I arrived in the big house's living room, only Juniper and Jude were there. Juniper was on Jude's lap, idly stroking his hair while Jude played on his phone. Of course, as a thirty-year-old man with two brothers-in-law, I shouldn't go feral when my sisters cozy up to their spouses. Still, I wanted to punch the guy.

Instead, I sat on the couch and pulled out my phone. "Do you know what we're doing?"

Juniper gave an exaggerated groan. "Seriously?"

"No, I'm kidding."

Juniper rolled her eyes. "We have our Segway tour."

I looked up from my phone. "Our what now?"

"Sedgwick's Segway Tour. It'll be great. We'll ride Segways along the bike path, ending in a fireside supper by the ocean. They threw it in with the rental."

So many thoughts blasted through my brain that I was temporarily speechless. Rubbing the back of my neck, I reminded myself I was here for family. Because, as the greeting cards say, family is everything.

Juniper knew what was about to happen and covered Jude's ears in mock protection—not that Jude noticed. "We're ready."

I'm not one to disappoint.

"What kind of pseudo-bougie establishment offers Segway tours to secure rentals?"

She giggled. "Maybe they're trying to get the buzz out on a new business venture."

"The Segway tour business? Who wrote that business proposal? And what self-respecting human being invested in it?"

Now, I didn't really care if some entrepreneur had decided to set up a Segway business. And provided there wasn't any photo evidence for future blackmailing, I would even ride one along the beach. Though it's extremely stupid, and I will stand by that till the day I die. What I really needed was an excuse to let off steam after my afternoon with Mom, my detective friend, and Miss Apricots. Thankfully, Juniper knew me well enough to get that, goading me just enough so I could go full tear until I'd worn myself out.

I hadn't noticed Mom enter until I was pausing for air. She placed a hand on my shoulder and said, "Nigel and Casey went straight to the van and packed up the kids."

Juniper gave Jude a final kiss before saying, "Have fun."

Juniper left, and Jude remained on the chair. "Here you go." And Mom tossed him the Corvette keys.

"Where are you going?" I asked.

Jude smirked.

"Where's he going?" I asked, following Mom outside.

"He's seeing some friends in Carentorrie."

I froze. How did Jude get a night off?

"Holt," Mom called. "Get in the van."

This is how most kidnappings start.

As it turns out, Segwaying was an adventure I would go on with only my parents and sisters. Nigel was tasked (or volunteered?) with driving the van with the kids to our campfire destination. While I had my doubts about the venture, no one ever considered leaving me alone with my niece and nephew. Of course, I love kids. Obviously, I love those cute little snot buckets. Still, to my great sorrow, the magical togetherness we spend is a rarity. Which is too bad, because as previously stated, I love kids and never find them the slightest bit annoying.

Sedgwick was a dude, maybe in his fifties. The second instructor was a gangly teen wearing a Dungeons & Dragons shirt. There I was. Stranded with a fantastic attitude, a helmet forced on my head, and a waiver signed saying I wouldn't sue for death or dismemberment. How often did dismemberments happen? Seriously, I don't know what's the matter with me. Arguing with Juniper should have done some good, but a black cloud still hung over me.

There was plenty of laughter and chatter from my mom and sisters as they learned to drive the things. The best I could do was grit my teeth and keep quiet. Unfortunately, I picked up steering the thing pretty quickly. Juniper pulled up beside me and said, "If you're too good, we'll think you ride them all the time."

She drove off before I had a comeback.

Here for family. Here for family. Segwaying for family.

What was my life coming to?

# A NOT SO SHOCKING MURDER

As soon as we reached the campsite, I unclipped my borrowed helmet and tore it from my head. Sweat had stayed locked in that medieval safety contraption, and I needed another shower. Running my hands through my hair, I did my best to slick it back so I looked less like Oscar the Grouch.

"Always so vain," Casey commented, already holding Baxter and Harper—her priorities were slightly different from mine.

I flashed her a charming grin. "As the final single person, I've got to do something to increase my chances."

"Because your dream is to get married and start popping out kids."

I looked her straight in the eye. "You know me. Can't wait till I'm a stay-at-home daddy."

"Mm-hmm." Casey wasn't convinced. "Well, you'll never catch a date with all that stubble."

"Hey, this is my vacation five-o'clock shadow, and I'll have you know many celebrities pull this off."

"Right. Because you and Ryan Gosling are basically twins."

"You said it, not me. Tap, tap, no take-backs." With that, I maturely walked away as every wiser older brother should.

For supper, we were served a meal of freshly caught fish and barbecue chips for the authentic taste of nature that makes the tourists go rabid. Once we filled our plates, Dad and I shared a large rock facing the small fire.

Who knows if Baxter or Harper ate. From what I saw, Nigel and Casey were running relay races, grabbing one kid from getting too close to the flames, then the other from getting too close to the water. What can I say? Children are a blessing.

Behind us, the Sedgwick's Segways crew began loading our rides into the back of a waiting truck. Since I was sitting with Dad, the only conversation I got was what drifted in from the other groups. Lucky for me, I was closest to the Segway crew.

You know how most people gossip about work or relationships? Well, in Amelia's Haven, they talk about murders. Seriously, this was bad. They spoke of murders like other people talked about the weather. A simple matter of course.

"No, Dad," the Dungeons & Dragons kid was saying. "The second murder was Death of a Yogi."

"Are you sure?" Sedgwick's voice was distracted.

I glanced at Dad. Was he hearing this? But Dad was too busy keeping his napkin from blowing away to pay attention.

The kid continued. "When do you think it'll be our turn?"

"Turn?"

"You know, like someone dies in a Segway accident. We're super sad. Detective Reynolds tells us it was murder. We start getting a lot of questions and hot cocoa from Dakota. Then, all of a sudden, we find out one of our closest friends is actually a coldhearted killer."

"Never." The voice was harsh. "Segway tours are never getting bit by murder bugs. I went through all that. It's why I left the town council and set up my own business."

"You would have been safer if you'd stayed. Think about it. The bug only bites a group once."

"The case was solved. Remember?" Sedgwick was ready to lay down the law. "As bizarre as it sounds, Carlson strangled the councilwoman in the last phone booth so the vote to remove it would pass."

The kid wouldn't let it drop. "And that doesn't sound crazy to you?"

"It became clear to me that politics, even the small-town kind, aren't for me."

"But what about…?"

"Tanner!" Sedgwick took a breath. "Just finish loading."

"Come on," the kid whined. "Haven't you noticed a new person decides to commit murder every few months, just when stuff settles back down?"

Sedgwick sighed. "Allen was new in town. The poisoning had something to do with his past."

I zipped my pullover up a couple more inches, suddenly feeling the need to hide the 10k logo. Hopefully, that idea wasn't spreading around town. Dakota and my cop friend had already implied plenty about my possible involvement.

"What do you think Allen was into?" the kid said. "It's Allen. He stared at birds and wore a fanny pack."

Sedgwick and his kid got into the truck's cab, and I couldn't hear anything else.

There was something very wrong with this town. Seeing Dad had his napkin situation under control, I asked, "Did you consider taking the family to Maui instead of here?"

A strange look passed over Dad's face. Was he terminally ill and not up for a long plane ride?

"We talked about it." He ate a chip, then looked at me. "It would take you at least a week to adjust to island time."

"Island time? What's that, three hours?"

"You know how you get."

Was Dad serious or seriously messing with me? I couldn't tell.

"And you didn't consult me?"

"We saw free Segway tours at Amelia's Haven and were sold." He flashed a grin.

"Dad!"

He winked.

Whatever my parents' reasoning, I was stuck in Amelia's Haven for a few days. With nothing better to do than wait around and hope I wasn't bitten by the previously undiscovered murder bug.

# CHAPTER 8

The sun was setting when we loaded back into the van. I was resting my eyes on the drive back when my phone vibrated. I ignored it.

It went off again. Still, I didn't bother checking. Then Juniper kicked the back of my seat. Sitting up, I turned to give her a piece of my mind. She widened her eyes and wiggled her phone at me.

A new message was just coming in from Juniper. It read: *Be cool.*

The first message was: *Movie at your place?*

The second one said: *Holt???*

Running a hand through my hair, I considered the question. I'd been planning on showering, updating my files, and turning in. The little quiet time I'd had was ruined by Dakota. Did Juniper think I'd let her invade my sanctuary of peace and quiet?

Sensing a *no* was coming, a new text came in: *I'll bring kettle corn.*

Glaring at my phone, I wondered when my sister would get old enough to stop being a pest.

I replied: *Butter or no deal.*

She sent the crying-laughing emoji. What did that mean? She'd better take my popcorn stipulation seriously.

As soon as we got back, I took a quick shower. When I exited the bathroom, it was to find Juniper perfectly at home on my couch. She'd brought two bowls of popcorn. One was butter. Maybe Juniper wasn't so bad.

"What happened here?" She had my laptop open and was reading the murder file. Juniper was that bad.

I grabbed my computer. "I'm working."

"On what?"

"What movie did you want to watch?" I asked.

"Come on, Holt. I didn't mean to snoop." Juniper made a pouty little-sister face. "I was going to set up a movie, but I saw the file marked *murder board*. Of course I opened it."

I sat next to her with a sigh. Mom already thought I was crazy. Was it so bad if Juniper did too?

"Did you read the part about DJ Hughes being murdered here?"

"He died in this garage?"

Yup, she thought I was crazy. "He died in a mansion a couple of miles from here."

"Since when were you a DJ Hughes fan?"

"I'm not!" I said a little too quickly. "Apparently, every few months, there's a new murder here. DJ Hughes was one of them."

"Are there that many people in town to kill?"

"Exactly," I said. "There has to be something going on here. I just don't know what."

"Did DJ Hughes 'Start this Game'?"

I began a slow clap. "His biggest fan, who knows all his songs."

Juniper continued, "Did he 'Control the Power'?"

"Stop it."

"Maybe I 'Can't Stop on Sundays.'"

Juniper received a pillow to the face.

There was muffled giggling under the cushion. Carefully, she peeped out. "Fine, I'll stop." When I didn't throw any more pillows, she sat up. "Have you watched documentaries about DJ's murder or the trial?"

By my dumb look, she knew the answer was no. "Holt, you can't survive on looks."

I winked. "At least I'm pretty."

Juniper took control of my laptop, and one rental later, we were watching, *The Murder of DJ Hughes.* Unfortunately, this account was more social media nonsense. His parents, friends, fans, and even an ex-wife who didn't hate him, were all weeping about his accomplishments and the legacy he left behind.

Juniper started skipping past anyone who was crying and all the long montages of fans losing their minds while he performed. We got through an hour of the documentary in fifteen minutes.

After one of my loud sighs, Juniper got defensive. "My idea's still good," Juniper said. "This is just the wrong film."

The fast-forwarding continued past a massive shrine full of flowers, music albums, and merchandise.

"Stop!" I jerked forward. A woman appeared on the screen who wasn't crying and had none of the glitz or glam of everyone else. Could it be the coroner? Juniper rewound, and we watched the homely examiner explain how the injuries were incongruent with a simple fall down the stairs. Rather, DJ Hughes had been hit over the head and was unconscious or dead when he fell, proving he'd been murdered.

Hard cut to more weeping.

Limos began filling the screen, stalling in front of a massive cathedral. Superstars began alighting in all black, wearing thousand-dollar pairs of sunglasses, but Juniper didn't fast-forward.

"Juniper?"

"What? I like her bag!"

The fast-forwarding could only continue once Juniper's fashion icon had entered the cathedral.

When my favorite detective flashed on the screen, Juniper pressed play. He started by saying Amelia's Haven had never had a murder since Sebastian Oglebee founded the town in 1889. Times certainly had changed. Sebastian would be proud.

My cop friend continued by explaining how evidence pointed to DJ's manager. Juniper was about to fast-forward when Dakota came on the screen, explaining how she'd been at the mansion that night because the power had gone out. She was resetting the breakers when the manager's car arrived, and yelling began.

I twisted toward Juniper. "Dakota told me she found him. She didn't mention she was the last person to see him alive."

"Interesting," Juniper said.

Nothing else happened in the remaining half hour.

Next, we tried a reenactment so low budget, the actor playing DJ Hughes didn't get temporary sleeve tattoos. Instead, he wore what was best described as women's tights Sharpied with strange designs attempting to be artsy. As the film progressed, the stockings kept snagging. Holes grew until his *tattoos* were actually removed for the close-ups of him lying at the bottom of the stairs.

Not much was learned from the reenactment. Instead of filming the ornate stairwell from the Caldwell Mansion, as seen in the documentary, they used the stairway from what I assume was their grandma's house.

The production was so bare-bones, I expected Dakota to show up playing herself. No such luck.

My eyes were watering, and I'd caught the yawns real bad. Still, I didn't object when Juniper switched to YouTube and began playing courtroom footage.

Clicking on the top views, we got a good overview of the case. The motive ended up being pure greed. Mr. Manager wasn't happy with the percentage of money he got from DJ Hughes and tried to renegotiate the numbers. DJ said something like, *If you're not happy with this, I'll find someone who is.* And that's all DJ wrote.

The sick part was Mr. Manager got a higher percentage of DJ Hughes's sales with DJ dead. Note to self, never be worth more dead than alive. While the case dragged on for months, the jury found Mr. Manager guilty in less than three hours of deliberation.

Partway through closing arguments, a hand on my shoulder had me opening eyes I didn't know were shut. Juniper smiled. "Good night, Holt."

"Mm."

Juniper turned the light out as she went. I wanted to make a joke about her turning the lights off when I was still in the room, but I couldn't get the words in the right order. Stretching out on the couch, I proceeded to *watch* more of the trial.

---

The blaring of an air-raid siren had me falling off the couch and landing in a heap on the floor. The shrieking continued as I tried to sit up. Everything was fuzzy, and it was hard to focus on anything but that infernal sound.

Was it a fire alarm? Should I go outside? I didn't see smoke, but the blaring was definitely coming from inside the room. I had one shoe on in preparation for my evacuation when I saw my phone vibrating on the sea chest. My alarm clock?

Tripping in my one shoe, I stumbled to my phone and shut the infernal noise off. My normal alarm was techno chimes. Juniper had swapped it for air-raid sirens. She had a death wish.

There was a text from her waiting: *Now you'll have time to shower.*

I sent the head-exploding emoji.

Juniper replied a second later: *Mwahaha.*

As important as plotting my revenge was, brushing my teeth was of first importance. That was a step I'd neglected last night, and I could tell. If I didn't hurry, Juniper would be texting to say she could smell my morning breath from the big house.

Once my teeth were cleaned, I hopped in the shower and tried to get the kinks out of my neck. Sleeping on the couch was much better than the foldout bed but not as good as home. But, ignoring the cramped neck, it was a decent night's sleep.

The hot water helped me focus. According to the documentary, no one had been murdered in Amelia's Haven prior to DJ Hughes's death a couple of years ago. And now? Allen had been poisoned in a diner, his friend had been struck with binoculars, and Brittany's fiancé had been stabbed at sunrise. Besides, the teens at the B and B had mentioned a trident killing, and

# A NOT SO SHOCKING MURDER

Sedgwick had been talking about a phone booth strangulation. Six murders, all starting with DJ Hughes.

These were just the murders I'd heard about in the two days I'd been here. Who's to say how many more bodies there were. And now I had my detective friend and Dakota acting like I was a suspect in Mr. FunRun's death.

Amelia's Haven is a small town. Statistically, how many murders are supposed to happen here? Whatever the *statistical* number, this gross town was exceeding it.

Banging my elbow against the shower wall, I groaned. Have I mentioned I hate Amelia's Haven? Even the name sounds dumb. And how many murders need to happen per capita before the entire town is abandoned?

Were the cases related? What were the odds so many people would catch homicidal fever? I, for one, don't believe in murder bugs.

The shower water was cooling, and I turned the heat up.

There was so much attention on the DJ Hughes case. It was literally the death of an icon. If Mr. Manager had been framed, his million-dollar defense team or the millions of people following the case would have proven it. And not to be a total Boy Scout, but he was found guilty by a jury of his peers.

It had to be a business deal gone bad. Dakota was just doing her job when she last saw the two of them together that night and was as surprised as anyone to find DJ Hughes dead. Mr. Manager was safely locked away. There's no way he could have shown up for the beachside murder. But was DJ's death a falling domino, triggering a deadly chain reaction far removed from the original crime?

Pounding on the bathroom door had me cowering in the shower and giving the most masculine scream the world has ever heard.

Was I next?

"Holt," Mom called.

I sagged against the wall. "Yeah?"

"Everyone's in the van waiting to go."

Huh. I really should find the schedule. What I said was "Sorry. Out in a minute."

Making fantastic time, I ran outside with damp, finger-combed hair. The van was already gone, but Dad was there, leaning against the Corvette, reading. He slid a bookmark halfway through *The Maltese Falcon* before closing the book.

"Your mom didn't know how long you'd be. She thought it would be best if we took two cars."

"That's awful."

Dad's eyes twinkled. "Exactly."

# CHAPTER 9

Turns out Mom had set up beginner surfing lessons. When we arrived, Casey and her kids were walking on the pier. Mom, Juniper, Jude, and Nigel were lying on surfboards on the sand, practicing paddling.

I had just showered.

Dad went immediately to an empty surfboard and began following along. I watched, running a hand through my hair. Sand was getting everywhere.

Somehow, Mom had scheduled the lessons for the first nice day. And by nice, I mean the sun was out, while the breeze held a kick. The ocean would still be chilly, and there was a pile of wet suits by the surfboards. Secondhand wet suits. Rented wet suits. Wet suits an unknown number of bodies had already squeezed into. Sure, I was here for family, but wasn't Segwaying enough?

"Holt," Mom called.

I needed coffee. "I'll go check on Casey."

Mom was on her stomach, boxed in by Dad and Juniper, making my getaway easier than usual. On my way to a coffee cart, I did say hello to Casey and avoided Baxter with his bright blue snow cone.

The coffee tasted how you'd expect it would from a beachside cart. Still, I was determined to enjoy it. Sitting on a bench just out of earshot from the surfers, I began sipping.

DJ's case had gone to trial. What about the other murders? How many arrests had been made?

After buying my second cup of coffee, I was returning to my bench when I checked on the surfers' progress. The lesson was on a break. Mom was marching toward me already in her wet suit, while the rest of the family was changing.

All of a sudden, buying a muffin became my top priority. The muffin excuse wouldn't be worth much to my mother, but all I needed was to stall long enough for the class to resume. Instead of getting the muffin, a much better opportunity in running gear was leaving the cart with a water bottle.

"Brittany," I said. Was I smiling?

"Holt." She gave a polite nod.

Brittany could withstand my charm, but would she help a poor soul in need? Mom was getting close. I had to act fast.

"Listen, remember how you saved me from an afternoon of finger painting?"

"Hard to forget."

"Right, well, would you take a walk with me right now? I'm trying to get out of a surf lesson."

The scar by her right eyebrow was now visible as she looked from me to my approaching mother. "All right," she said.

"Great. Let's go now."

We started walking down the boardwalk. She began drinking her water, while I sipped the cheap drip coffee. I forced myself not to look behind me. My fate was already sealed. Mom would catch me after the lesson. I couldn't hitchhike to Seattle.

"You don't surf," Brittany stated.

I decided it'd be best to keep my thoughts on communal wet suits to myself. So I gave a roundabout answer. "It's not like I took a vow not to. But it's a surf lesson with my family, first thing in the morning. I don't want to flail around in the sand."

There was a strange choking sound. Brittany was trying not to laugh…again.

I grinned, something I did a lot more when I was around her, and we continued walking in comfortable silence. Me growing smarter with every gulp of coffee.

I definitely liked Brittany's workout clothes better than her uniform…not that there was anything wrong with her uniform. She'd be sexy in a potato sack. Brittany must've been partway through a run because she was a little winded with a slight sheen of sweat across her face.

"You're staring."

I cleared my throat. "Sorry."

Brittany's mouth quirked. "You're sorry you got caught."

"I never like getting caught."

We'd faced each other, our eyes dancing. Then her hand lifted to tuck a piece of hair behind her ear. The glint of the diamond had me taking a step back. She dropped her hand, and we continued walking. This time the silence was uncomfortable.

I frowned. Maybe I should stop flirting. I could ask her about the investigations. She'd know which cases had and hadn't gone to trial. Problem was, I didn't want to milk her for information. She'd rescued me from two family outings and deserved better. Besides, I didn't want to hear her talk about the murder of the love of her life.

Daring a peek at the surf lesson, I could see they were now splashing the surfboards around in the ocean. But I didn't feel safe returning. What does one say to an almost widow?

The silence stretched.

*Say something. Anything. Make a joke or comment on the weather.* If only I could think of a full sentence.

Brittany beat me to the punch. "What have you heard?" she asked.

"So much," I said before thinking of anything better.

Brittany's face fell.

Sighing, I took a seat on a bench and was glad when she followed suit. "After yoga, a lady in a wig told my sister about…" I trailed off, finding it difficult to get the words out.

"My brother being in jail for killing my fiancé?"

"Yeah." I glanced over at her. She looked fine. She'd probably had this conversation so often, she'd become immune. "When you said Allen was helping you, was it in clearing your brother's name?"

Brittany watched a wave roll in. "I know my brother didn't kill Jeremy. It never added up. When Allen came here for a birdwatching trip, he had a similar experience. His best friend was accused of killing his girlfriend and then making a run for it."

A shiver ran through me, even with the sun shining. Without thinking, I asked, "What happened to your…?" Why couldn't I say the word *fiancé*?

Before I could figure out why, Brittany began answering. "Sunrise yoga was Jeremy's idea." Britt's face had a pained softness to it. "He told me after we got engaged that it started as an excuse to spend time with me." She gazed into the distance like she saw the past. "When he first invited me, his excuse was on the East Coast he was used to doing sunrise yoga and he intended to keep doing it, even though in Oregon the sun rises above land."

Well, wasn't Jeremy romantic.

Brittany shook her head. "I should have been there. We always met for an early warm-up before everyone arrived. I was walking over when the mayor collapsed in his yard from a heart attack. I was at the hospital when I had a chance to call Jeremy and tell him why I hadn't shown up." She grimaced. "Dakota answered the phone. Then, a week later, Paul was arrested."

"Could I talk to your brother?" Where had that come from? Why talk to a murder suspect? What if he'd done it?

Brittany was analyzing me, similar to how she'd looked me over in the ambulance. Again, the little scar was very apparent. This time she was deciding whether I was a crazy tourist or a sexy man of intrigue.

"Sorry," I said. "From what I've heard, Amelia's Haven has had a murder problem since DJ Hughes." Knowing I couldn't sound much crazier, I continued. "I think there's a connection."

The color drained from Britt's face. "Could be," she said.

"Is your detective worth anything?" Another thoughtless question.

"Some people think he is" was her careful reply.

Trying to lighten the mood, I leaned in closer. "If you ask me, all that cop could catch is a case of cooties."

Brittany's eyes widened before she threw her head back and laughed. That wasn't what she'd expected. Hopefully, I wasn't what she'd expected.

Schooling her face, Brittany said, "His timing was unfortunate. We ran out of cootie shots right before Detective Reynolds joined our department."

"Blasted budget cuts."

She shook her head. "Can't do anything anymore."

As nutty as it was, I was about to ask again if I could speak to her brother. But Brittany started talking, "Koa's classes usually wrap on the hour."

Right. Of course, the surfer's name was Koa. No one with a boring name like John or James would teach surfing lessons.

"Well, Britt"—I stood and offered her my hand—"thanks for the rescue."

She accepted my hand, her eyes sparkling. "Careful. You're almost behaving like a gentleman."

I tried not to grin as I asked, "Would it help if I tripped you?"

Britt just shook her head.

We'd just started walking when she asked, "Did you call me Britt?"

"Um, no?"

Had I? At least it wasn't something weird like *Miss Apricots* or *Mr. FunRun*. Britt was a shortened version of Brittany.

She nodded in mock seriousness. "All right. 'Cause if you had called me Britt, I'd need to ask why."

I grinned. "Good thing I didn't."

The walk back to my family was shorter than I remembered. Brittany and I continued our easy banter, but now my family was not-so-subtly watching.

Britt noticed. "Is it uncommon for you to talk to women?"

"No," I said, pretending I wasn't about to shoot my family with a death glare. "It is uncommon for them to be close enough to watch."

"Well, let's show them you've got game."

Suddenly, Brittany had placed a hand on my biceps and was throwing her head back, laughing.

"They'll expect you for Christmas," I grumbled.

Britt winked. "You're welcome." With that, she resumed her run.

Juniper was the first to reach me. "Wasn't she at yoga?"

"What did you say to her?" Casey asked.

"Yes, to Juniper. And, Casey, with a face like mine, I didn't need to say anything."

"Did you hire her to impress Mom?" Casey asked.

Juniper jumped in. "Struggling small-town actress thought she'd landed her big break when—"

"That's enough," Mom said, a little slow to the party.

I smirked while Juniper and Casey stood with their hands caught in the cookie jar. Or so I thought. Then Mom added, "She's not an actress. She's his paramedic."

Casey and Juniper began talking over each other, at first too excited to hear Mom's juicy details. The trio went down to our bus, prying apart my business.

Dad was waiting, and we walked to the Corvette together. "Your mother and sisters can get carried away," he said.

I nodded, glad he was my ride.

"But after today, I think you should know your grandmother wanted you to have her wedding ring when you're ready to pop the question."

I groaned, and Dad chuckled.

# CHAPTER 10

Midafternoon was scheduled free time while Casey was doing her mother-child bonding time.

Replaying the conversation I'd overheard with the teenage waitress at the haunted doll B and B, I remembered the time frame she mentioned for the poisoning. If that was accurate, Baxter making me spill my coffee might be one of the unluckiest moments in my life. That incident left me bumping into Mr. FunRun during the poison window.

Had the waitress said how many people had paid their bills in the poison window? I'd been facing the register, but either I was staring at a seahorse or Allen. I knew what the back of Allen's shirt looked like, not who paid their bills.

Had his drink already been poisoned when I knocked into him? I didn't kill him, but had I almost saved him?

I could ask the waitress a few questions. Would the waitress be working a shift at The Dining Seahorse? The Victorian brunch place would've closed a couple of hours ago.

Was I actually planning on going back to The Dining Seahorse? If I was returning to that tacky death trap, I better be taking the Corvette.

Dad was reading on the patio, and I decided to get him in a good mood before asking for the keys. "What's your book about?"

After giving me a long look, Dad said, "It all starts when PI Sam Spade's partner takes the case of finding a mysterious woman's missing sister. Spade gets called out of bed when his partner's found dead that night. That's the setup for a much more complex story. I could fill you in. Read you my favorite sections." Dad began playing with the Corvette keys, daring me to ask follow-up questions.

My jaw ticked, but Dad's stare never wavered.

"Fine." I sighed. "Yes, the real reason I'm here is to borrow the Corvette."

Dad tossed me the keys. "Not a scratch."

I sighed again. Dad had been saying that since I first got my learner's permit. "Not a scratch," I repeated.

Keys in hand, I was ready to return to the scene of the crime. Great.

I didn't speed on my way to the diner. If anything, I drove under the limit. My heart was beating extra hard, and my hands were moist around the steering wheel. But it was fine. I could go back to that place of death and nightmares.

At the parking lot, The Dining Seahorse's garish sign stared down at me. Was a flock of seahorses called a murder?

I stayed in my car for a few minutes, waiting for my heart to slow down. If I were more attuned to my emotions, I'd consider what this unease meant for my psyche. This failure was why my college girlfriend Tasha (a psych major) broke up with me. That was actually a calming thought. I'd gotten this far by shoving stuff deep, deep down. Why stop?

Telling myself I was fine, I headed into The Dining Seahorse. If I got too messed up, I'd lie on a couch and tell Juniper my problems. Otherwise, I could ask Mom or Casey to fix me. Dad would solve the problem with a pat on the back and a book recommendation.

Since murder is bad for business, the diner was predictably emptier than it was on Tuesday. I chose a barstool on the opposite side from Allen's stool. Next, I ordered lemonade from yet another guy in high school. What are the current labor laws for teens?

I sat there sipping my lemonade, trying to ignore all the grinning sea monsters. So far my waitress hadn't appeared. She was working at two restaurants. Did she ever get a day off? Glancing over at the waiter, I tried to think of a non-creepy way of asking, *Is that young waitress working today?*

I was sipping on my second lemonade, and I still hadn't come up with a non-predatory way of asking about her. It was becoming increasingly likely she wasn't working. A text came from Juniper. One so long I almost didn't read it. Especially since it started with an explanation about her brand and platforms and why she'd been somewhere during her free time, doing something with strangers.

I skimmed the message so quickly, she could have slipped in her social security number, and I wouldn't have noticed. But at the end was a poem her new friends had taught her. A shorthand Amelia's Haven's teenagers had come up with to keep track of the murders.

> The manager's anger turned red,
> And DJ Hughes was found dead

# A NOT SO SHOCKING MURDER 87

> Jeremy lay in Corpse Pose,
> From which he never rose
>
> When the phone cord went tight,
> The councilwoman saw the light
>
> Binoculars for birding,
> Found a new use for hurting
>
> A trident's bite,
> To end someone's night
>
> Bad deeds still brewing,
> Allen starts spewing

At the end of the poem, Juniper included several emojis of Sherlock Holmes's hat. At least she's humble.

Me: *That's the worst poem I've ever read.*

Juniper: *You're welcome.*

I was figuring out my reply when my waitress appeared, waltzing through the kitchen doors. She gave my waiter a little wave, and he winked back.

"Hey, Bea," the waiter said.

Hold on. Wasn't she part of a love triangle? Could she be dating a kid from each restaurant? I looked for his name tag. Carlos. Had I heard that name? Was he the midnight serenader?

In my excitement, I swallowed lemonade down the wrong pipe and began coughing.

All I got from Carlos was a casual "You good, buddy?" But my waitress screamed and dropped her notepad.

"Bea, are you all right?" Carlos reached for her.

"Yes…I, uh…excuse me…" With that, Bea picked up her notebook and ran back into the kitchen.

"Bea?" Carlos followed her out.

I waited. Those creepy glassy-eyed seahorses peering down at me. The place had given me the heebie-jeebies before Mr. FunRun died. Glancing at my phone, I found a message from Mom, reminding me I was running low on free time.

When Carlos reentered, I started my intrusive tourist act.

"Excuse me," I said, making my voice obnoxiously loud so Bea would hear me.

Carlos came over. "Another lemonade?"

"No, thanks. I was actually wondering if you knew where a good romantic spot was." There was no movement from behind the door, so I laid it on thicker. "I got this guitar and was hoping to—"

The door swung open. Bea appeared, looking mad. "Carlos, can you reach the extra napkin dispensers from the top shelf?"

"Uh, sure." He gave me a shrug before going back into the kitchen.

I didn't know what to expect when Bea made the first move. Hands on hips, she marched up to the counter. "Do *you* have a problem, or do *we* have a problem?"

Okay, Bea was super cool. Not only did she have the work ethic to have two jobs, but she also had the energy to date two guys.

Bea popped a hip. "Supposedly murderers like returning to the scene of the crime. Is that what you're doing?"

# A NOT SO SHOCKING MURDER 89

"What? No!"

She made that disgusted face only teenagers can pull off. "From what I heard, Dakota made you hot chocolate." Bea tossed her hair. "I assumed you were the killer."

"I think we started off badly. I'm Holt." She stared at me like I was an alien. "I was wondering who paid their bills in the window of..." I frowned. In all that time sipping lemonade, I hadn't figured out a non-suspicious way of asking who the other suspects were.

There was a *no* forming on her lips when Carlos made a reentry with two napkin dispensers. She giggled. "Did I say dispensers? I meant extra creamer. Do you mind?"

He gave a goofy grin. "I misheard." And he was gone again.

When she turned to me, any semblance of a smile was gone.

Leaning against the counter, I said, "I'm team Carlos."

"Whatever." She rolled her eyes. Hard to tell what was real disgust versus being a bratty teen. "Beyond a few regulars, there was one couple on their honeymoon."

Who would choose to honeymoon in Amelia's Haven?

Trying not to look nauseated, I asked a follow-up question. "Who were the regulars?"

A voice boomed from behind me. "Just us."

I twisted around, and there was my detective friend, along with Soccer Dad and Brittany. Miss Apricots was also there. She wore a watermelon dress and stood so close to the detective, their arms were almost touching.

You know the best thing about Seattle? You can be in a packed café full of strangers who ignore you.

Carlos came back out and went to the register. "Ready?"

Soccer Dad went to pay, and after a quick shrug, Brittany followed. My detective friend looked like he wanted to say something, but Dakota placed a hand on his arm. "I've got this," she said.

The cop gave me a good glare before moving to the register.

Dakota's fake smile was so wide, most of her teeth were visible. "I didn't think you'd come back here," she said.

Mirroring her smile, I shrugged. "Best lemonade in town."

"Is that so?" Her voice had an edge, like I was encroaching on her territory. Realizing her perfect Realtor mask had slipped, she batted her false eyelashes at me and took a step closer. "I would hate if one of my renters was pestering hardworking townspeople with strange questions."

I tilted my head. "Oh, okay. Can you remind me why you stopped by my place yesterday?"

She gave a light laugh. "Didn't I say? The grill needed to be checked." Miss Apricots was a cooler customer than the detective.

"Right," I said. "Must have slipped my mind."

Dakota and I sized each other up. A spark passed between us. Confusing. I wasn't attracted to Miss Apricots. Right?

"Time to go," the detective barked. He was in an extra-bad mood. Maybe Dakota was standing too close to me.

The group trooped past me, with the detective holding the door open for Miss Apricots.

"Are they dating?" I asked the waitress.

Bea raised one shoulder. "Depends on the week."

"Interesting. Well, thanks for your help." I flashed a winning grin, and Bea gave me a glare that would kill a weaker man.

Making friends everywhere he goes—Holt Jacobs.

# A NOT SO SHOCKING MURDER 91

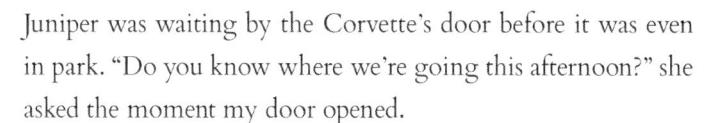

Juniper was waiting by the Corvette's door before it was even in park. "Do you know where we're going this afternoon?" she asked the moment my door opened.

"Of course I don't."

"Here, I highlighted it for you." Juniper shoved a paper in my face.

At first it was hard to read, because Juniper's hand was shaking like she was an overexcited puppy. Then I read it.

*Sand Museum.*

Only my mom could find a Sand Museum. It wasn't even in Amelia's Haven. We had to squish into the van and drive twenty minutes to a neighboring town. But Mom assured us—or assured me—it would be worth the trip.

My expectations were very low. Still, I didn't expect an out-of-business fast-food restaurant converted into a museum.

According to Mom, the other sand museums she'd gone to were full of sand sculptures. Unique works of art that Mom found captivating. This museum had pictures of children's sandcastles. There were various containers filled with samples of different types of sand, with details explaining the different sediments. And that was just the first exhibit.

Also, the building was the size of a regular fast-food restaurant. Mom had budgeted ninety minutes in a space that, at best, could have occupied us for thirty.

With forty minutes to go, I was hanging out in the room that had once been the children's play area and had been updated to be a room dedicated to the history of sandbags. I was hiding behind a display of 1950s sandbags, checking my phone, when someone entered. A quick glance showed Juniper instead of Mom.

I was returning to my phone when Juniper said, "Isn't the *Allen spewing* poem great?"

Frowning, I said, "Calling it poetry is a bit of a stretch. How do people tell you that stuff?"

Juniper crossed her arms. "If you'd bothered to read the whole text, you would have seen the explanation."

I gave her a blank stare. She should know I don't read itineraries, and I don't read long messages full of self-gratification.

Juniper rolled her eyes. "Whatever. Really I think the only reason they told me was that the teens had just figured out Allen's verse and were proud of the newest edition."

"The only improvement to that poem would be forgetting it."

"Again, you're welcome. Now you have a list of all the murders in Amelia's Haven."

She had a point. I shrugged, not wanting to admit she was right.

"A group of them came up with the rest of the poem while waiting to give their statements after the trident killing," Juniper said.

"What trident killing?" And there was Casey.

I really didn't need more people weighing in on my theories. Besides, I generally try to keep unnecessary scary information from parents of young children.

Juniper had no such qualms. "There was an aquarium fundraiser where a woman was stabbed to death with a trident."

Maybe it would be all right if Juniper kept the other deaths to herself. A second later, Juniper was reciting the entire poem from memory, detailing the deaths from DJ Hughes to Allen.

Casey tilted her head. "If the Allen in the poem is the one who died in the diner, that man had a heart attack."

If Juniper could just keep the poisoning to herself…then it wouldn't be Juniper. The next moment Juniper was detailing the poisoned sweet tea.

"So there's been six murders, starting with DJ Hughes? That was only two years ago."

I nodded.

"Does Mom know?" Casey asked.

"I tried to bring it up." I shifted on my feet. "It didn't go too well."

Casey's eyes grew distant as she thought through the information. Then came an unexpected smile. "It sounds like the Ocean Cove Mysteries."

Should that make sense? I looked at Juniper. She shrugged, as clueless as I was.

"You know," Casey said.

We shook our heads.

"The TV movie mystery series."

Still nothing.

"Based on some author's book series."

Did Casey think this information was helping?

"Well…" She looked between us like she couldn't believe we didn't know what she was talking about. "The Ocean Cove Mysteries take place in a tourist town. Izzy Nixon runs a frozen yogurt shop. She begins solving murders when her business partner is found dead, locked inside the walk-in freezer. While the handsome cop originally suspects her of the crime, they begin working together, start dating, and by the end of the movie, solve the murder. There's tons of sequels, all with murders in this supposedly idyllic town."

Juniper's eyes lit up. "That's exactly like this!"

I frowned. "Well, instead of a frozen yogurt owner, the female sleuth is Mom's rental agent, who shows up randomly with hot cocoa."

"Hot cocoa?" Casey wrinkled her nose.

"If the teenage waitress is to be believed, Dakota bringing me hot cocoa means I'm a marked man."

"I wouldn't worry about it." And for a moment, Casey was a responsible mother of two. Then she bit her lip, and there was a crack of the kid I'd grown up with. "It's not like she's dating the local detective."

I grimaced.

"Oh." Casey's eyes widened. "Really?"

"Yup," I said.

Casey shook her head. "Well, that certainly checks all the boxes."

Juniper tried to make a serious face. "You'd better be worried. There's no hiding from Dakota, the hot cocoa sleuth."

# CHAPTER 11

When I opened the door to my room that night, I was met by a blast of heat. What had happened? Why was my room ninety degrees?

I'd woken up to an air-raid siren. Had it been warm then? It was hard to say. But it had been comfortable the night before with Juniper.

Juniper. I didn't know how, but it was absolutely her fault. Time to give her a quick call.

"What's up?" Juniper asked. Her cheerfulness was extra annoying, given the oven I was standing in.

I skipped any pleasantries. "Juniper, why is my room so hot?"

There was silence on the other end of the line.

"Juniper?"

When she did speak, her voice was as close to apologetic as it ever got. "I guess I forgot to turn off the baseboard heater after our movie night."

"Juniper!"

She squeaked out a quick, "Sorry," before ending the call. Probably for the best, given how irritated I was.

My room had baseboard heating? Since when? I found the baseboard on the third wall. Turning it off was easily done, but there remained the problem of my room being a sauna. I tried leaving the door open, but garage fumes of spilled gasoline and oil began wafting into my room. Also, I wasn't confident downstairs was mouse free. Closing the door, I looked for alternatives. The big picture window above the couch didn't open. However, a further inspection showed an ancient AC unit jammed in the bathroom window that had previously been as ignored as the baseboard heater.

The AC was so old, it might do nothing besides cough up smoke and die. Still, my shirt was sticking to me, and I was desperate enough to give the relic a try. Rancid smoke didn't seep from the machine, but a fine layer of dust and allergens were kicked up, causing a bout of sneezing.

Draping a sheet across the couch, I lay down in nothing but my plaid boxers. I didn't bother closing the curtains to the window above me. Sure, the dumb thing was sealed shut, but being able to look outside made the room less oppressive. The door to the bathroom was open, encouraging the breeze to reach me where I lay, looking up at the moon. Settling in, I wondered how long before I'd fall asleep in the heat.

The thing is, I woke up later and couldn't figure out why. There had maybe been a crash. I was definitely in pain. My room was still dark. It had to be the middle of the night. When I tried to move, daggers of pain tore through my skin.

If forced awake, I'm more zombie than human. When I returned from my German study abroad, I could have been declared brain-dead for the first half of winter break, even with Mom's coffee and Dad's winter walks. This was one of those times. I couldn't get my bearings. I couldn't quite remember where I was. When I scratched at something on my chest, it bit both my hand and rib cage. For an insane moment, I wondered if the murder bug had gotten me.

Growing increasingly frustrated, I did what any self-respecting adult would've done—I called my mother.

She picked up on the third ring. "Holt?" Her voice was tired, but she was still more alert than me.

"Something's wrong," I said. "I don't know, I just woke up, and everything hurts."

She was getting out of bed and murmuring something to Dad. Then she said, "Okay, I'm on my way."

Lying still, I took a deep breath. So relieved my mommy was coming to the rescue.

Suddenly the lights were turned on, and I was convulsing from the shock.

"Holt? Holt?"

Something was definitely wrong.

"Holt!"

Was it my turn to answer?

"Yeah?"

"Stay still. Okay? I'm calling 911."

That seemed an overreaction.

My eyes must have closed because suddenly Dad's voice was in the room. "What happened?"

Opening my eyes, I did something I should have done earlier and looked down at myself. Aside from wearing only a pair of plaid boxers, I was bleeding from cuts along my body.

Mom was simultaneously talking to Dad and on the phone. "…shattered all over him…"

What now? My eyes were shut again. *Pull it together.* Had my window broken? Struggling to check, I saw air where glass used to be.

Trying to sit up brought more stinging and Mom telling me to stay still. I lay back, this time not even trying to keep my eyes open.

Next thing I knew, Britt or Brittany was there, bending over me. "What have you gotten yourself into?"

I blinked at her, not quite sure why she'd be in my bedroom. Was this a dream?

"Can you talk?"

Could I talk?

"Does he take sleeping pills?" Brittany asked.

"No," Dad said. "Not a morning person."

*Thanks, Dad.* I wanted to say something witty about it being the middle of the night but came up empty.

"Hey, stay awake," Brittany said, touching me with her gloved hand. "Come on, open your eyes."

How were they shut again?

"Listen up, Holt," she said as I managed to blink at her. "We're going to clear the glass away, then bring you to the ambulance to finish the check-up."

Her eyes were so brown. And there was that little scar. Could I touch it? Then a partial memory came to me. "I'm not wearing pants." I tried to get up, but Dad was at the head of the couch and held my shoulders down.

"Not now, champ."

"Pants?" I repeated.

Britt had been talking with the soccer dad EMT but turned back to answer. "Right now you're wearing glass. When we take that off, you can put clothes on."

Was she hiding a smile? What were the chances Brittany would see me being such a mess twice in one week?

Taking a pair of tweezers, she began removing shards from my skin, with Soccer Dad holding a dish for her to drop the pieces into.

A thudding began. At first faintly, then growing louder, until the grouchy cop appeared at my doorway and began stomping through my room. Must he be so noisy? He started talking to uniformed officers I hadn't noticed before. "Has the scene been secured and photographed?"

"Yes, sir. Plenty of photos."

Hold on. Will there forever be *plenty* of photos of me lying almost naked, barely conscious, and covered in glass?

A groan escaped.

"Sorry," Brittany said. Was she talking about the piece of glass she'd removed from my torso or also horrified by my new modeling career?

The cop marched over to where I lay. "What exactly happened?"

I blinked at him.

The detective waited. I stayed silent and staring. He glanced over at Brittany. "Is he on something?"

She shook her head, and again I got the impression she was trying not to laugh. "His dad says he's not a morning person."

Okay, it was still dark out. Probably three a.m. The fact they were all up and annoyingly energetic spoke more about them being psychopaths than me being on something.

Dad shook my shoulder. "You should answer."

I was staring. Maybe an improvement on closed eyes?

"Well, Officer—"

"Detective."

Did he want me to answer?

Dad squeezed my shoulder. Fine. I'd be the bigger person. "O good wise sir, keeper of peace, ruling the lands with law and order—"

The copper looked at Brittany. "Can you give him something?"

She ignored him, tweezers easing a shard of glass from my abs.

"Come on, Holt," Dad said.

Didn't my parents realize I'd kept myself alive without their help for over ten years? I only get a few death threats and a reasonable number of hate notes around the holidays.

"Holt?" This time it was Britt.

And my eyes were shut. Fantastic.

Pulling myself together, I answered, "What do you expect? I fell asleep and woke up to a broken window. I didn't see anything. I didn't hear anything. Because—and let me repeat this—I was sleeping. Which is the normal thing to do in the middle of the night."

The detective's neck had turned a blotchy shade of red. His mouth opened and closed a couple of times before hanging open. Was he counting to ten?

"Thank you, Mr. Jacobs," he finally said.

"Why are the police here?" I yawned. "Isn't this faulty installation? Like one of those act of God deals?"

My cop friend held up an evidence bag. "This brick was used to smash in your window. On one side, it says *drop this*, and on the reverse, *or I drop you.*"

A brick had been hurled through my window? Who would do that? And why?

"Does that mean anything to you?" he asked.

I closed my eyes, trying to think. A sigh escaped, and I was being shaken. Okay, I'd play along.

"*Drop this, or I drop you?* What am I being dropped from? They've already dropped a windowful of glass on me. What else do they want?"

The red on the detective's neck crept up to his cheeks.

I wasn't trying to be difficult. I was just a poor zombie trying to kick-start the day without caffeine. And how does *drop this, or I drop you* make any sense?

Brittany decided to save the situation by separating me and the detective. "All right, Holt. You and I have a date with an ambulance."

"Is this a date where I'll need pants?"

Britt's mouth quirked. "No, but we'll get you some shoes."

I made it to the ambulance without making a bigger scene. My dad and Soccer Dad stayed behind, talking with my detective friend. Mom met me by the ambulance with a mugful of coffee. "Drink up."

Yes, ma'am.

Maybe it was the coffee or the fresh air, but some brain fog cleared. Mom left, so Brittany and I were alone out there. I began watching Britt as she worked. Glass was still getting removed, and now there was an ointment and whatever that Band-Aid tape stuff is called being applied to my skin.

She noticed my attention. "Are you awake enough to answer a couple of questions like a normal person?"

I grinned. "Oh, I'm never that awake."

She shook her head. "I was afraid of that. Seriously, though, are you good?" She frowned, before rephrasing, "How's your pain level?"

"Trust me. I'm fantastic." Then I fought off a yawn.

Britt's mouth quirked. "You're going to fall asleep as soon as we leave."

"If not sooner."

The moment we were having (if you could call it that) was broken by Miss Apricots showing up in her watermelon ensemble. Something unspoken passed between her and Brittany.

"Holt," she called a little too loudly. How was everyone so cheerful at this hour? "I heard what happened. I'm so sorry. I called David, my window guy. He said it was the middle of the night, and he wouldn't fix the window until morning but promised to do it first thing. I made a pot of hot cocoa, which is heating in the kitchen, and I left your mother with a gift certificate to The Marina. Would you like to spend the rest of the night at the motel while your room gets fixed?"

It was too many words to process. I ended up saying, "Uh, thanks."

"Now, what happened?" Dakota asked.

Brittany snorted, pushing a piece of glass deeper into my thigh. I flinched, causing even more damage.

"Oh, Britt. I didn't see you there," Miss Apricots cooed.

"Right." Brittany's whole body was rigid. "Why don't you head up? Detective Reynolds will be far more helpful than Mr. Jacobs."

"Um, the motel?" she asked, a little flustered.

My eyes flicked up to Brittany. "I'm good here."

"Well, let me know if you change your mind. You have until daylight." She gave a laugh that was supposed to be cute and went upstairs.

This was a time to keep quiet. Whatever their deal was, it was none of my business.

Brittany shook her head. At first she didn't say anything. Just kept working, with the scar by her eyebrow the most defined it'd ever been. Finally, she sighed and met my eyes. "You know those people you grow up with, who are always there, but you mostly get used to them, and then your fiancé is murdered, and they're suddenly butting their heads in places they really don't belong, crashing a funeral, pestering your nana until she has a stroke, before pinning the whole thing on your twin brother, Paul?"

I blinked at her. There wouldn't be a good answer to that one if I were fully rested, and what I said was, "Uh…"

She gave a sad smile. "Go to sleep, Holt. Try not to remember anything."

I hadn't noticed she'd removed the final shards and put on the last Band-Aid.

It was the perfect time to say something kind or appreciative. What actually came out of my mouth was a yawn.

She laughed. "That's what I thought."

"Thanks," I managed.

She nodded.

Waking up the next morning, I had the strange feeling I was being watched. Blinking, I found Baxter staring at me.

What was Baxter doing in my room? I sat up and winced, the pain bringing it all back. I wasn't in my room. I was on the couch in the big house, which meant the night before wasn't a nightmare.

"Why's your pillow wet?" he asked. "Were you peeing from your mouth?"

I sighed. Baxter was waiting. "No, kid. That's drool."

# CHAPTER 12

Going up to my room, I scanned for damage. But the room was eerily the same as before. There were no obvious signs of last night's chaos. A new windowpane glinted in the sunshine. Was Dakota's window guy done? It wasn't even seven a.m.

Had it all been a dream? If my hundred new paper cuts weren't enough proof, there was a faint scent of silicone in the air. A closer inspection showed tape stuck along the edges of the new window, and the glass was shinier. The sheet I'd slept on was missing, along with the brick and glass shards.

*Drop this, or I drop you.* Had I really been threatened?

"David was here at five thirty, when the police were heading out."

I hadn't heard Dad come up the stairs and swallowed a yell. He held two cups of coffee and handed me one. I took a sip. It was much better than the one from the beachside coffee cart, but I missed my Seattle brews.

I sat down, staring numbly at the sea chest.

"Found any more shards?" Dad asked.

"Nope."

He sat next to me with a sigh.

"What happened last night?" I should know the answer, given I was the starring player.

"Nothing much." Dad took a drink. "The detective grumbled about you. They took a lot of notes and pictures before leaving."

My eyes wandered back to the sea chest. It was empty. Was something missing...or different?

"My laptop?"

"Right." Dad yawned. "I brought it to the house."

"Thanks."

Was the missing laptop the reason the back of my neck was tingling?

I glanced over at Dad. His head was resting against the couch, and his eyes were glazed. He'd dealt with a lot of my drama last night. I really shouldn't bother him. Still, I couldn't shake the feeling something was off.

"Was anyone else up here?"

"Hm?"

"You know, besides the police, Dakota, and the window guy."

Dad stretched and stood up. "Only your paramedics."

My cheeks heated. I wanted to say, *She's not my paramedic.* But Dad said *paramedics*, which included Soccer Dad. He hadn't meant anything romantic. I was the one jumping to conclusions.

"Dakota stopped by with fresh cinnamon rolls," Dad said. "You can help yourself. We're supposed to be at the van by nine."

My stomach roiled. Usually, I would have jumped at the chance for fresh cinnamon rolls. However, I normally eat healthier meals, and this week my diet consisted of sugar and grease.

"I'm good."

Dad nodded.

I rubbed a hand across my face. "How bad was I last night?"

"Better than Christmas, worse than New Year's Eve."

I groaned. "Well, that's something."

Dad clapped a hand on my back before heading downstairs, chuckling.

Brittany must think I'm an idiot. Not that it mattered. I was leaving Amelia's Haven after Mother's Day.

---

Back home I'm a regular at the gym. Living on Mom's schedule and eating junk this week left little time or energy to exercise…unless yoga counts.

I don't know if sunrise yoga is a daily thing in Amelia's Haven, but it was too late regardless. Besides, if Brittany was there, it would be impossible to concentrate. With plenty of time before nine o'clock, I put on sandals and shades before heading out for a walk. It should've been a run, but walking with tons of tiny cuts was uncomfortable enough.

Why would anyone bother threatening me? I was a tourist who'd be heading home in a couple of days. All I'd done was ask a few questions about Allen and the recent murders. Just like Allen had. My feet slowed. Were these the exact steps Allen had taken before he'd been killed?

Everything I'd done, all the questions, had been in public places. Anyone could have heard. Besides, it was a gossipy small town. Most of the population probably knew about last night's incident with the window, and those who hadn't were still in bed.

According to Dad, the only people in my room were Dakota and the first responders. Just like Allen's death.

Well, I'm excluding the teenage waitress and the window dude. But could I take them off the suspect list? They could be in cahoots. I don't know why a waitress and a window installer would decide to murder a retired birdwatcher, but dig deep enough and there might be a reason somewhere.

I was walking on the left side of the road, which gave me plenty of time to get out of the way of oncoming cars. From behind, a car approached, then slowed. It began driving at the speed I was walking. I kept going without looking in the vehicle's direction. People do strange things, and it's generally best to ignore them.

Then there was a quick whine of a police siren. It was my cop friend. Detective What's-His-Face was leaning out the window, watching me.

Perfect.

Had the guy moved to Amelia's Haven because he'd annoyed everyone else in the bigger towns, and this was his last chance at law enforcement?

"Morning," I said.

Skipping any pleasantries, he went straight to business. "Did you remember any new information from last night?"

"Nope. Any arrests made on my assault case?"

His eyes narrowed. "What assault? It was vandalism."

"The window was vandalized, and when the glass cut me into a hundred little pieces, it became assault."

"Next time, sleep on a bed."

*Let it go. He's a dumb jerk. Just let it go.*

I didn't let it go. "Are you saying it's my fault because I slept on the couch? Like I should have known this would happen?"

A flush was working its way up his neck. "Um, well, no. I mean, all of Dakota's rooms have beds, so it's assumed the renters use them. I didn't really mean that you…" He started twitching, and I'm sure he was counting in his head. He probably hoped I'd jump in and say something to rescue the conversation. Like I was the type of person who'd do that. If he were counting to himself, he would have made it to fifty before he finally said, "My apologies, Mr. Jacobs. We'll continue investigating."

"Thank you," I muttered.

He rolled up the window and peeled away, leaving me with the lovely scent of burning rubber.

I continued the walk through my cop friend's metaphorical dust. Reaching Amelia's Haven's tiny downtown, I was going to head back to the rental when Juniper called my name. She sat with Jude outside a cutesy café, eating a breakfast free of Harper or Baxter crying.

When I got to their table, Jude gave me a nod before pulling out his phone and beginning to scroll.

My phone vibrated. "Did you just text me?"

"No," Juniper said, also checking her phone.

Mom had sent a message on the group text. Were we late for something?

Instead of a text saying we needed to get our butts in the van, it said: *Dad resting. The morning is now free time.*

My legs went a little shaky. Mom canceled the morning because Dad needed to rest. Swiping a chair from an empty table, I took a seat by Juniper and frowned down at my phone.

Now I wished the text were about us being late for some obscure tour at some unknown place no one cared about.

How had Dad been? He'd been quiet. More than usual? When does your father change from the giant who wrestles with you until you *almost* pee yourself into an old man?

"Holt!"

"Hm?"

"What's wrong?" Juniper asked. "Do you have a toothache?"

"No."

"You look like you have a toothache."

I sighed. "I told you something was off with them. See." I waved my phone in her face. "Mom canceled…"

"Shuffleboard."

"Sure. She canceled shuffleboard because Dad needed to rest. Tell me again how both our parents are in the peak of health."

Juniper made a face. "He needed rest after being up all night with your window problem."

"Oh."

"Yeah, oh."

Juniper darted forward, trying to muss my hair. I dodged. Her momentum continued, and she was about to fall off her chair when Jude caught her arm and pulled her back. She giggled up at him.

"Thanks, babe."

"Try not to make a scene," I said.

Juniper winked at me. "I've missed you."

The crazy part is she meant it.

Being as smooth as always, I had the perfect reply. "Um, I…well…uh…"

Juniper's eyes darted past me, and she grinned. "You should leave."

"What?"

"Go!"

I still had no idea what was going on as I replaced my chair. I'd taken a couple of steps when I understood Juniper's excitement.

"Brittany," I breathed.

Did that sound creepy? Or like I was trying to be weirdly seductive?

"Holt." Brittany gave me a thorough once-over before asking, "Are you awake yet?"

"Barely."

Her lips quirked. "Do you remember last night?"

I shrugged. The memories were all jumbled. More like a dream where not all the pieces fit together. "Well," I began, "I wasn't wearing pants."

She tried to frown in an attempt to hide the smile. "You were very concerned about that."

"I didn't want you to get the wrong impression."

"Clearly," she said. "Do you remember anything else?"

"That cop dude stinks. Like I'm not into all the hippie-dippy stuff Juniper is, but his chakra or whatchamacallit is off."

"He said the same about you."

Trying to look offended, I bent in conspiratorially. "You know, it's a wonder he ever got that job."

"Right." Her dark brown eyes were searching mine.

I ran a hand through my hair. "What's up? Did I say something dumb?"

"No." She shrugged. "I did."

She did? Racking my brain, I came up empty. "Dakota came by," I said, trying to jog my memory. "There was tension. You didn't like her in school, and then she gave your nana a stroke at…" Horror played across my face, followed by a foreign desire to hold her hand and say I was sorry. But Britt's face showed she'd gotten enough pity to last a lifetime.

I leaned closer. "If you ask me, whatever's wrong with the detective's chakra, he must've caught it from Dakota. You think you're so great at managing rentals? Don't have windows that shatter when bricks hit them."

It was a joke, but Brittany's face remained serious. "Did you mean what you said yesterday?"

What had I said?

She continued. "About visiting my brother, Paul?"

"I think so." It was an honest answer, though not particularly polite.

Brittany nodded. "With all the excitement last night, I didn't know how much more trouble you wanted. Allen talked to Paul a couple of weeks ago, and look what happened."

For some reason, when I stood close to Brittany, it was hard to remember last night's threat or Allen's murder. Her black hair gleamed in the sunshine. I would've agreed to any scheme that let me spend more time with her.

"Holt?"

I was staring. Clearing my throat, I asked, "When should we go?"

"If you're free, we could go this morning."

I grinned. "Lucky for me, shuffleboard was canceled."

While we walked to Brittany's car, she filled me in on the details surrounding Paul. His case hadn't gone to trial yet, and with bail denied, he was housed in the Carentorrie Jail.

What crime shows leave out is how much of a pain in the derriere it is to visit someone in lockup. I'd never been to the Carentorrie Jail. While Brittany could more or less waltz in, I would have to fill out a dictionary's worth of paperwork, which included signing away the rights to my firstborn child. To sweeten the deal, there was a chance I wouldn't fill out all the forms before visiting hours ended, or I might be denied access if I forgot to dot an *i* or cross a *t*.

Carentorrie was about an hour away. We'd already be cutting it close, but one look at my shorts and sandals and Britt was informing me I had to change. Jail (like private school) had a dress code.

Brittany drove us to the rental, and I jumped from the car and rushed to my room. I'd packed a couple of pairs of pants. Slacks for Mom's fancy dinner tomorrow night and a pair of jeans. My dress pants were hanging up, and I had to empty my suitcase to get to the jeans.

I was too busy hurrying to remember all the cuts on my legs. Wincing at the sudden pain, I nearly lost my balance. The only positive was no one saw it happen. Grabbing a pair of socks to put on in the car, I stuffed my feet into running shoes and left my room.

Charging downstairs, I almost collided with Mom.

"Where are you going?" she asked.

"Jail," I blurted before thinking of something that sounded better.

"Okayyy." She dragged the word out. "Do you remember our boat ride to Captain's Point at twelve thirty?"

Of course I didn't. Was I even given an itinerary? "Sure," I said, sliding past her. "It's just a quick errand."

Mom was skeptical.

"It has to do with the guy at the diner," I said.

That threw her, and she took her time figuring out her next question. "Is this something you need to do for…closure?"

"What? No! I'm fine. I'm good. This isn't a trauma thing."

"Well, you did experience quite a shock, and it would be understandable if—"

"I'm good."

"Right." She didn't believe me. But when would my mother really think I was all right?

"Brittany's waiting. I really have to go."

She nodded. "You're released."

I was already at the door when she called, "Holt."

"Yeah?"

"I love you."

I froze with my sunglasses half-on. "I know…I love you too." And with that, I was in Brittany's car, and we were leaving Amelia's Haven, heading straight to jail.

# CHAPTER 13

My hand was cramping by the time I got through all the forms. I could have bought a house with a thirty-year fixed mortgage with less paperwork.

Britt had been with Paul since our arrival. Once I was approved as a visitor, I was escorted into a large visiting room with metal tables and attached stools.

I didn't like the pain on Brittany's face. Was this all a big mistake? What could I do? I wasn't a private investigator. Would it be better if I didn't get involved? She spotted me where I stood hesitating and gave me a nod.

Taking a seat next to Britt, I tried not to stare at Paul. It's not that he looked deranged or anything. Still, the man looked nothing like Brittany. His hair was tangled and reached to his shoulders. He also sported a beard in need of trimming—nothing like the sexy stubble I was rocking.

"Holt, this is my twin brother, Paul."

How were they twins?

"Hey." I held out my hand before wondering if I would get yelled at by a guard for touching.

Paul gave me a quick handshake, and no one yelled or wrestled us to the floor. So far, so good.

"Brittany tells me you're the newest tourist visiting Amelia's Haven." A spark flashed in Paul's eyes. Those brown eyes were Brittany's. With some grooming, maybe this could be Britt's male duplicate.

Freezing, I wanted to nudge Britt under the table, but the fear of yelling guards or eating a faceful of concrete kept me still. "What did you tell him?" I asked, trying to keep my voice calm.

Brittany tried to look innocent, but her twinkling eyes gave her away. "Only the highlights."

"Right."

Did Britt tell the story where I had her give my mom a sick note? Paul winked when he caught me trying to figure out what he'd heard.

"Holt?" Brittany's voice cut through my thoughts.

"Hm?"

"Was there something you wanted to ask Paul?"

Hadn't there been a reason for coming? I had to focus.

Running a hand through my hair, I went for it. "I've found the number of murders in Amelia's Haven suspicious. I was hoping to hear the details of your arrest. The police haven't exactly been eager to help."

Paul's eyes turned tired. "You realize Allen came here with similar questions and then was murdered in the middle of a crowded restaurant?"

Not what I expected. But I tried to be nonchalant. Shrugging, I said, "We already made the drive."

He nodded slowly. "All right." Paul took a deep breath. "It all seemed routine at first." He glanced over to Brittany. "Horrible but about what you'd expect. The cops went around asking us questions about where we were at sunrise and the last time we saw Jeremy. It started getting weird, though. Dakota Willows started popping up with food and hot cocoa. Why hot cocoa in July? She was asking all these questions and acting like she was just being neighborly. But that ship sailed after the prank she pulled on Brittany in high school."

We both turned toward Brittany, but she gave a slight shake of her head. Paul continued with his story, but I made a mental note to ask Britt about the prank.

"Dakota was there at the reception after the graveside service. Again she was asking lots of questions that weren't any of her business, and my nana got so upset she had a stroke. Brittany had to save Nana the same day she buried her fiancé."

Brittany's scar was noticeable. Otherwise, her face was a professional wall nothing could penetrate.

"A couple of nights later, I had a blackout. I'd planned on going out on my boat to fish. Maybe I did. I don't know. No matter how hard I try, the last thing I can remember is getting dinner at The Marina. Then, somehow, I'm on my boat, getting arrested, with Dakota unconscious in front of me." While his voice didn't waver, his hands were beginning to tremble. "Dakota says she was going to ask me more questions, and the next thing she knew, Detective Reynolds was reviving her in my boat. The cops said I kidnapped her and was going to kill her because she knew what I'd done to Jeremy. I didn't kill him. I couldn't. I wasn't anywhere nearby. And I'd never take Dakota." The tremor in his hands grew worse. "I just don't remember what happened."

I decided to ignore his anxiety and stick to the facts. "Were you tested for drugs?"

He shrugged. "They dragged their feet on that. It took forever to get a lawyer and even longer to get a drug test. If I was drugged, it was out of my system before the test."

The lights in the visitor room flashed. "Time to leave," Brittany said, shifting to her feet.

I also stood, but I had one more question. "Where were you during the murder?"

"The night of Jeremy's death, I was night fishing. The GPS should show I was at sea, heading home for the day. But I was alone, and Detective Reynolds said I could have brought a smaller boat or spoofed the GPS. Like I know how to hack."

I nodded. "Thanks for taking the time." I shook his hand again and left the room so Brittany could have a private goodbye.

Her eyes were glassy when she showed up in the lobby, but the stoic expression remained.

---

We sat silently in the parked car. Brittany hadn't turned it on, and I was in no rush. Clouds had rolled in while we were in jail. Is that symbolism or just the Oregon Coast?

Something glinted from the cupholders in the middle console. When I looked over to see what it was, a silver band with a glittering diamond blinked up at me.

"No jewelry in jail," Brittany said. She picked up her engagement ring but didn't put it on. "Almost everyone in town thinks Paul did it. But I know he didn't." She shook her head. "That's not proof." Her fingers tightened around the ring. "Some people think I'm too naive. Too close to Paul to see what he's done.

Others think I know my brother killed Jeremy, and I want to cover it up. Like I'm choosing my brother over my fiancé. Wearing the ring is the best way I can think of to show I still care for Jeremy. But"—her eyes shot briefly to mine—"I'm ready to put this behind me."

I wanted to have a serious conversation with every single person who could misjudge Brittany so badly, and it wasn't just to get the ring permanently off her finger. "I'm sorry you have to make those decisions."

"I don't know what to do with this case," Britt said. "I never did. One day I went from having the ideal life with a great family, an awesome job, and Jeremy. To losing him, having the police ask me and my family all sorts of questions, Dakota butting her nose in places it didn't belong, and, for the crowning achievement, my brother getting arrested." She shoved the ring on her finger and clenched the steering wheel. "It shouldn't make a difference, but Dakota's private investigation still irritates me."

I didn't reply. Saying something generic like *I'm sorry* was too cheap, and I couldn't think of anything particularly deep.

The quiet remained as she began to drive through Carentorrie. Who knows how long the silence would have stretched if my stomach hadn't growled…loudly. I was hungry but not about to starve. I'd been doing my best to sit respectfully in silence, but my stomach decided to announce I'd skipped breakfast, and it was now lunch.

A strangled sound came from Brittany. One look from me had her bursting with laughter.

"Are you hungry?" she asked when she could get air.

"Kind of. I'll make a sandwich when we get back."

The grip on the steering wheel loosened. "I could eat a burger."

"Yeah?"

"Yeah," she said.

I grinned like we were going to the prom.

It wasn't until I was halfway through a terrific mushroom Swiss burger at a truck stop diner that I said, "Once in high school, I forgot to wear pants to school. I was so embarrassed."

"No, you didn't."

"Maybe not." I drummed my fingers on the table. "Let's see. This was really embarrassing. I wore the same shirt as a buddy of mine for senior pictures."

"How humiliating."

"It was the worst." I paused, but Britt didn't jump in. "Now I've shared an embarrassing story. It's your turn to tell me something embarrassing from your past. Say…high school."

She shook her head but was amused instead of moody. "Okay. So this isn't as bad as a matching shirt for senior photos…"

"Oh, nothing's as bad as that," I said.

Britt's mouth quirked. "Clearly. But for a much less embarrassing story from high school"—I leaned forward expecting something extreme—"once I was wearing white shorts, and Dakota poured a bottle of apple juice on me and told everyone I peed myself."

"Uh." I cleared my throat, a little confused.

That was it? That was Dakota's prank? The one Paul had implied made them lifelong enemies? It was mean…but there's a chance I'd done a couple of worse pranks in my day.

I sat back. Not quite sure what it meant.

Was Britt hiding something?

# CHAPTER 14

Since I didn't voice my suspicions, the drive back was a peaceful affair. There was a drizzle so light, Brittany didn't bother with the windshield wipers. My phone had stayed in the car for my jail escapade, and I hadn't bothered checking it. Halfway through the drive back, I noticed it glowing. Casey's name flashed across the screen. I clicked ignore. The phone lit up again. This time Juniper was calling, and I clicked ignore for the second time in a minute.

When I unlocked my phone, I found thirty-nine unseen texts, seventeen missed calls, and messages from any social media profile my family had access to—including a LinkedIn account I'd forgotten existed.

What time had Mom said I needed to be back by? I'm guessing I missed the boat.

The phone rang again. It was Dad. I was trying to maintain some semblance of being cool in front of Brittany, and my family wouldn't leave me alone. My game is so much better when I'm alone in Seattle.

"Something important?" Brittany asked.

Groaning, I slouched in my seat. "Remember how I needed a doctor's note to get out of finger painting on the pier?"

"Yeah."

"Well, I kind of went MIA on a boat ride, and they're freaking out."

Brittany's mouth quirked. "If you're sure it's not an emergency."

I went from being annoyed to having sweat form along my temples. When Jude's number appeared on the screen, I answered before the second ring. "How's Mom?" I asked.

"Having fun yet?" Unsurprisingly, the voice wasn't my quiet brother-in-law but my annoying baby sister.

I wanted to lower my voice so Britt couldn't hear, but I was sitting shotgun in her car. No matter what she pretended, there was no way she didn't hear everything I said.

"Are Mom and Dad okay?"

"Yes, Holt, they're fine. You're the one who went to jail. Can't we be worried about you?"

"I visited the jail. I wasn't admitted!"

I winced. What was my problem? I'd just described Brittany's brother.

Taking a deep breath, I did my best to regroup. "Juniper," I said through gritted teeth. "Please tell me there was a reason for all the missed calls that doesn't include me going to jail."

"Oh, that."

"Yes, that."

She giggled. "Are you white-knuckling the phone?"

"Affirmative."

Squirming in my seat, I tried to be patient while waiting for the giggling to stop. Instead, I heard, "Give me that." And Casey came on the line.

"We're fine. The excursion boat broke down, and we're stranded at Captain's Point. Nigel didn't take his allergy pill and left his inhaler in our room. Can you get them and bring them to us?"

"Sure," I said. Casey wouldn't be asking if it wasn't important. "I'll figure out how to get there."

"All his stuff is in the gray bag on the dresser. Bring the whole bag."

Sitting up straighter, I said, "Okay. We're getting close to the house. I'll be there as soon as I can."

"Thanks."

"Yeah," I said and hung up.

Britt noticed my shift. "Everything okay?"

Shrugging, I said, "Kind of. My brother-in-law needs his inhaler."

"Needs it or *needs* it?"

A grin spread across my face. "I don't think 911 will be called."

"All right." She shrugged. "I am working this afternoon. He could help fill my quota."

"Hey, I've done my part in fulfilling your quota of injured idiots."

"You have a point."

I rolled my eyes, then turned toward the window so she wouldn't see the heat in my cheeks. So much for suave and debonair. Talking to my sisters had ruined the vibe in the car. Nothing like medical emergencies to put a damper on the afternoon.

Brittany pointed at a side road we were passing. "Caldwell Mansion is up there."

"I've heard it has amazing views," I said before wishing I'd been less generic. I scrambled for something more interesting to say. "Was DJ Hughes's murder the only one to go to trial?"

Brittany took her time answering. "I guess so. Paul's arrest was next, and I didn't pay too much attention to what happened after." She thought for a moment. "My aunt is neighbors with Councilman Carlson, the phone booth strangler. She loves updating everyone about what he does on house arrest." Her lips twitched. "He's started binge-watching *The Golden Girls*."

*The Golden Girls?* How long had he been confined to his house?

"Let's see," Britt said. "Allen's birdwatching friend who killed his girlfriend with binoculars escaped before being arrested. They'd need to find him before they could try him."

Hadn't there been another one? I tried to remember the poem Juniper sent me. The only line I came up with was *Allen starts spewing*. Not helpful. I knew that one all by myself.

Brittany narrowed her eyes. She could tell I hadn't moved on. "The last arrest was for the trident killing at the Atlantis-themed fundraiser. That happened in February. I doubt there's even a court date."

"Was Allen at the fundraiser?"

"Probably. The whole town goes. The aquarium fundraiser is one of our biggest events all year."

Could Allen have seen something?

I frowned remembering my return to The Dining Seahorse. "What were you doing with Dakota yesterday?"

"Oh." Britt wrinkled her nose. "That was Detective Reynolds's suggestion. I think they're dating. He's always making excuses to spend more time with her. He claimed Dakota should join our work lunch because she had firsthand knowledge of Allen's death."

"Hm," I said. "My invitation must have gotten lost."

"Definitely. The only person Reynolds would want to see more than his girlfriend is a tourist he finds extremely annoying."

I grinned. "That's what I thought."

Huh. Was I in trouble?

*I like this woman.*

A few minutes later we were at the house, Brittany stayed in the car, scheduling my boat ride, while I ran inside to grab Nigel's junk. I also ran into my room in the garage to get a light raincoat. So far Amelia's Haven was free of raindrops, but the clouds loomed overhead, and I didn't want to take any chances.

This hadn't been a date. When we weren't eating, or in the car, we'd been in jail. So why was I disappointed it was ending? Would she have wanted to come on my rescue mission if she wasn't working this afternoon? Having Brittany as my tour guide for Captain's Point would have been something.

"There'll be a boat ready to take you," Britt said when I returned with Nigel's bag. "I have the councilman's number. If you'd like, we could give him a call."

"Uh, sure." What was happening to me? I actively avoided meeting new people.

Brittany pressed a few keys and turned the phone on speaker. As the phone rang, she pulled out of the driveway. The guy was under house arrest; surely he could pause binge-watching *The Golden Girls* long enough to answer the phone. There was a click, and I figured it was going to voicemail. Instead, there was a cranky "Hello?"

Brittany made it only partway through her explanation of why she was calling when the former councilman cut in. "Absolutely not. The only person I talk to about the case is my lawyer. I made an exception for Allen, and now he's dead. So tell your friend to forget about this, or he'll be next."

The line went dead.

Was that a threat? Did he think I'd be arrested or killed?

Brittany had flushed, and her mouth was opening to say something.

I cut in. "He's charming. I bet he donates all his time and money to charity."

Sitting back in her chair, Brittany let out a sigh. "Something like that."

"Why did he get house arrest and Paul's in jail?"

Britt's mouth ticked. "Because fishermen have less sway than town councilors."

At the dock, she introduced me to a scary fisherman who'd be bringing me to Captain's Point in a speedboat. The hulking man was also one of her cousins. However awkward I would have been saying goodbye, it was even worse with him watching.

"Uh, thanks," I said, wincing at how bland that sounded.

"Sure thing." I caught a twinkle in Britt's eyes before she turned away. I wanted to find out what she was thinking, but Nigel and, more importantly, Britt's huge cousin were waiting.

---

The boat roared across the ocean, and it wasn't long before a multilevel tour boat came into view, next to a strip of land that resembled the rest of the Oregon Coast. The magnificent Captain's Point. It truly was forgettable.

Casey forced a smile as she met the boat. "There you are," she said.

"How's Nigel?"

She looked behind her to Nigel lying on a bench. "He's fine."

"Hey, buddy. How you doing?" I asked when I reached him.

"I'm fine," Nigel wheezed as he sat up.

Clearly.

I shouldn't have stared, but *shouldn't* and *didn't* are two very different things. Casey and Nigel were a well-oiled machine. First, Casey had the water ready for the pill Nigel was popping. Next was a nasal spray, and she was there with a tissue. Then, for the grand finale, Casey had shaken Nigel's inhaler when it was time to take a puff.

"You're here," Mom said, walking up with Harper on her hip.

Dad was behind her, with Baxter on his shoulders, and gave me a nod of acknowledgment—love you too, Dad. Juniper and Jude were a couple of steps behind Dad.

"Did you bring any sandwiches?" Juniper asked, scanning me for food.

"No, Juniper, I was too busy saving the day to make a food stop."

She raised an eyebrow. "So you haven't eaten?"

"Children," Mom said, walking back from Britt's cousin in a tone that stopped all squabbling. "Ian said he could take a few of us back."

Who was Ian?

Mom was still talking. "Casey's family should go. The kids can take naps, and poor Nigel can recover. The boat should be fixed for the rest of us in a couple of hours."

Wait, was Ian the boat guy? My boat guy? Was I being stranded?

"It's my boat," I blurted.

Mom frowned.

"And it's a good thing it can fit Casey's entire family," I added.

"Come on, babe, let's go." Casey took Nigel's arm and boarded, while Mom and Dad secured their grandchildren in life jackets before depositing them in the boat. The motor revved and then jetted off. Leaving me stuck on some dumb Captain's Point.

"It won't be long."

I jumped and swallowed a yell.

Dakota Willows was standing beside me. How long had she been there? And how had she snuck up on me, given how strong her perfume was?

"What?" she asked. "Is there a bug in my hair?"

"Um." Without a better explanation, I began peering into bouncy beach waves that smelled too strongly of product to be natural. Today she was lemon themed. First, a ginormous plastic lemon was clipped in her hair, and she wore a blouse covered in them and matching yellow capris. "No bug," I said. "Just some fruit."

"Good." She flashed me one of those *friendly Realtor* smiles before facing my family. "Did you all see the caves?"

"We were told they were closed," Mom said.

"Oh, that's just because 'technically'"—Dakota made air quotes—"you need a guide to go inside. There's been no replacement since Mikey broke his leg."

Seeing the horror on our faces, she laughed. "Bike accident. It's not like he fell down a crevasse. Come on. I was a guide in the summers during high school. I guarantee there are no crevasses."

Mom and Dad decided to stay near the tour boat—to make sure it didn't drift away. If I were alone, I wouldn't have followed my landlord inside a set of shut-down caves. But I wasn't alone. I was with Juniper.

Apparently, before I'd arrived and Dakota had offered herself as a guide, Juniper had done her best to talk Jude into illegal cave exploration. With Dakota promising no crevasses, Jude just shrugged—Juniper's followers loved her adventures. As much as I didn't want to be trapped with Dakota, I felt an obligation to tag along. Also, if a rock fell on my head, I'd get to see Brittany again…and that was a seriously messed-up thought.

It was a short hike to the cave's entrance. The only thing stopping intruders from entering was a single chain strung across with a NO TRESPASSING sign hanging in the middle. Only honor or fear was preventing people from going in.

"Don't worry," Dakota said, stepping over the chain. "They only say that so if you get lost or injured, you can't sue."

Well, that was comforting. Had Brittany worked any dismemberments?

Since this was an unplanned excursion, we used our phone flashlights instead of headlamps. Juniper and Jude went on ahead, with Dakota sometimes calling to tell them which way to turn. Occasionally, Jude shone his light on Juniper, and she recorded herself, explaining how dangerous this latest exploit was to all her clamoring fans. Meanwhile, I was stuck, strolling along with Dakota in a dark cave.

"Remind me, have you been to Amelia's Haven before?"

A shudder ran through me. "Definitely not."

She ignored the snark, immediately moving on to her next question. "Then how did you know Allen?"

Stopping, I turned toward her. We were in a narrower section of the tunnel, so I bent my head lower, standing extra close—like we were about to kiss.

My brow wrinkled, her big eyes taking me by surprise...Were they too big?

"How?" Dakota asked.

"Hm?"

"How did you know Allen?"

"Right." I straightened, breaking the trance and banging my head against overhead rocks. I managed not to yelp and recomposed myself to actually answer her question. "We already had this conversation." I let my voice turn hard. "If you recall, I didn't know him."

"Okay," Dakota said in a singsong voice and started walking.

Did she think I was lying?

"I've been here for less than a week. What makes you think I knew Allen?" I asked, catching up with her.

"You've been awfully interested in his life for a perfect stranger."

I groaned. "Your detective already spoke to me. He can verify everything I've said."

Dakota beamed, like dating my cop friend was something to be proud of. "Reynolds refuses to tell me about ongoing investigations. I have to go on my gut, and it's telling me you wouldn't be so interested in the case if you weren't involved."

"What about you, Dakota Willows? You're awfully interested. How well did you know Allen?"

"I didn't," she mimicked.

"I know you knew him."

"Of course I knew him!" She laughed. "I know all the locals and half the tourists."

I stumbled back when a curl of hair fell in my face. For a horrifying second, I thought a cave creature was attacking. After fixing my hair, I tried to resume our conversation. "Then what were you arguing about before he died?"

"He wanted to renew his lease. I told him the owners were returning. He wanted me to get an extension. Now, Detective"—Dakota's voice bounced down and around the cave—"I've answered your question. Time to answer mine. Why do you care what happened to Allen?"

I turned to her. "Are you interrogating me?"

"Are you?" she asked.

"Are you?" I repeated—not above acting like a kindergartner.

Dakota straightened. "What if I was? What if I'm good at solving murders?" When I didn't reply, she harrumphed. "You've talked to Brittany. She's probably told you all about how I was a terror in high school and now I'm nothing but a snickerdoodle-baking gossip."

"Hot cocoa."

"What?" For the first time, Dakota was actually confused.

"Nothing more than a *hot-cocoa-making gossip*."

Her eyes skittered around the caves as she figured out a response. Finally, she shrugged. "Who doesn't like hot cocoa?"

We continued in silence, but my hot-cocoa-making sleuth couldn't let one thing go. "So you actually didn't know Allen?"

"Right. I actually didn't."

"Then why are you poking your nose into this?"

I wanted to ask her the same thing. Maybe get really close to her again. Only this time, I'd tuck the hair behind her ears, and…Hopefully, there was a toxic gas in the cave that was messing with my brain. I actively disliked Dakota as a person. Being even mildly attracted to her was way too confusing.

"Why, Holt?" Dakota prodded when I remained silent.

Why was I poking my nose into this? Clearing my throat, I decided to go with a partial truth. "Because he died in my arms."

Dakota laughed, and any attraction I'd felt evaporated. "Technically, he died in my arms."

Right. All I did was perform CPR on a corpse.

# CHAPTER 15

A blare on a horn echoed through the caves, summoning us back to the boat. After our walk in the light of phone flashlights, the glare outside was almost more than my sunglasses could combat. The sun was hidden, but the way it illuminated the clouds was pure headache fuel. And to make the day even better, it had begun raining. At least I'd brought my raincoat and was able to protect my hair.

When we reached the dock, Dakota went off to mingle with other people, and I could relax a little. Mom was midconversation with a pseudo-official holding a clipboard. She was explaining how I was on the list but hadn't made the trip out, and I'd been swapped for my sister's family. The official seemed bored and irritated by our little intrigue. I nodded on my way past and slipped into the boat.

Trying to find the place with the least people, I wandered through the different levels until I found the perfect bench hidden in the back corner of the boat. My safe haven. Then Mom sat down beside me. Had I packed headphones? Could I put on music and pretend to sleep?

Mom hadn't looked at me, but I could feel her disapproval. After a pointed reminder, I had missed a prescheduled outing and hadn't answered my phone until an hour later.

Sweat began forming on my forehead. "How much trouble am I in?" I asked. "Will Santa put me on the eternal naughty list?"

Mom waited until a bead of sweat rolled down my temple. "What did your voicemails say?"

"Uh, I haven't listened to them." I swallowed. There were like twenty missed calls. How many of them had voicemails?

"You can delete them. The first half were when we were trying to track you down. We stopped calling once I figured out where you were. The other half was about the boat breaking down and Nigel needing his medication."

Erasing the messages, I was slow to process everything Mom had said. "Wait. How did you find me? Are you tracking my phone again?!"

"Calm down." Mom sighed like I was being melodramatic. "It's quite simple. The jail told me you were still there. Adding the drive time back to Amelia's Haven, there was no way you'd make it back before the boat left."

"Mom, it's a jail. They don't just give out visitor information."

Silence from Mom.

"Right, I forgot." I removed my sunglasses and rubbed my eyes. "You're like the CIA. There's nothing you can't discover."

Mom continued her explanation like nothing had happened. "Once I knew you weren't lying in a ditch somewhere, we continued on with our scheduled afternoon."

"Super." Sliding my sunglasses back on, I crossed my arms and rested my head, assuming I would be given a reprieve. I was wrong.

"What does a broken window have in common with a trip to jail?"

*Brittany*. But I couldn't say that out loud.

When I didn't reply, Mom gave me a nudge. "I'm glad you called me last night."

I shrugged. "Who else?"

Mom went to find Dad long before we docked. I discovered the downside of my hideaway was I ended up being the last passenger off the boat. Casey had returned to the parking lot with the van, ready to drive us back to the rental. I was still stuck behind exiting groups as my family was loading up. When I had a clear path, the thought of getting back into the van full of weird smells from seven adults and two young children left me walking slowly.

Halfway across the parking lot, a voice stopped me. "Are you Holt Jacobs?"

I groaned. I'd been in town for less than a week. Was I becoming a local? How could anyone commit murder in Amelia's Haven with everyone watching?

Composing myself, I turned around to face a middle-aged woman. "Yes, I'm Holt."

"Sorry, I…" She shook her head. "I'm Allen's sister."

"Oh." That wasn't the correct response. But what was?

"Anyway…" Her hands were fidgeting. "I'm here to make arrangements for Allen and his things. I heard what you did." She looked me straight in the sunglasses. "Trying to save him. Thank you."

I nodded and decided it would be appropriate to remove my shades. "I did what I could." When she didn't reply, I tried small talk. "I heard he'd been here for only a couple of months."

She scratched at her neck. "The trip was supposed to be a week. Then there was a…tragedy, and he decided to stay longer."

I tried to look interested, but I'd heard it all before. The tragedy was the birdwatching bludgeoning, and he stayed to investigate.

She sighed. "Allen was so excited about his true-crime book."

I'd been eyeing the van, suddenly wishing to be safely inside and away from strangers. Her words caught my attention. "His what now?"

"Allen's book. He'd always wanted to write one. Then, after the…tragedy, he began looking into the town and said there was a story here."

Was anyone in earshot? I scanned the parking lot, but I didn't see Dakota. Was she the type to hide behind parked cars? Otherwise, the only people watching were in the van. I wasn't known for making vacation friends—though a grieving sister to someone I'd never met doesn't count as a friend.

Her lips trembled. "He always wanted to write. After retiring, he finally had the time."

I nodded gravely. Not wanting to scare her off, I tried to keep the excitement out of my voice. "May I get a copy of his book?"

"Um…I guess so." She shrugged. "Why not?"

"Great!" I grinned before remembering my manners and schooling my face to look somber. "About the book, how can I get a copy?"

"Right." Her attention had wandered. "Uh, Allen would email me drafts each week to back up his work. If you want, I can forward it."

Allen's sister was my new favorite person.

"Thanks," I said.

I gave her my email, and his latest draft was forwarded to my inbox with a few short keystrokes.

It was time to politely excuse myself. I was about to do that when there was a flash of red hair wearing yellow in the distance. It brought up another question. "Did the locals know he was writing the book?"

She shrugged again. "I don't know. Allen interviewed a lot of people. I assumed they knew what he was working on."

Interesting. Why had no one mentioned it?

"Well, thank you," I said.

We did a strange bow-wave thing at each other, and then I set off for the van. Right as I got to the door, the sun broke through the clouds and Amelia's Haven turned from gray to gold. When I got in, everyone was waiting expectantly…or everyone excluding Jude, who was on his phone.

"Who was that?" Juniper asked.

I climbed into the back row, sitting between the empty car seats. "I don't know her name."

In unison, my family shouted, "Holt!"

Sliding my sunglasses back on, I didn't dignify them with a response. Why bother with her name?

# CHAPTER 16

With all the excitement of being temporarily shipwrecked, Mom decided we'd have a quiet dinner at the beach house. All fine and good in theory. The kitchen was fully stocked with pots and pans. However, besides cereal and Dakota's cinnamon rolls, there wasn't much anyone would consider food.

Mom and Casey began discussing meal options on the drive back. They were still working out the perfect plan fifteen minutes later. In the end, Dad and I went on a secret shopping mission and grilled hamburgers. Halfway through supper, Mom and Casey were still planning the perfect home-cooked meal.

Juniper sat on Jude's lap while they shared a plate. Baxter managed to squirt ketchup all over my shirt. Dad continued reading *The Maltese Falcon* once he finished eating. While Mom reminded me the whole evening of my failure to appear for the tour and how important it was I be dressed and ready for tomorrow's formal dinner.

All was well in the world. For the first time since Tuesday, I was able to let all the Amelia's Haven drama hit the backburner. Soon I'd leave this awful town. And as long as everything was all right with Mom and Dad, things could return to normal.

Who had I been fooling? I was a random tourist in the wrong place at the wrong time. There didn't need to be a big conspiracy. I was stressed about the family vacation and would have been traumatized after eating at The Dining Seahorse with or without a dead guy. Maybe I should ask Mom to fix me.

By the time I made it to the garage apartment, it was dark, I was yawning, and the rest of the family was turning in. I'd managed to talk myself out of my newfound life as a private investigator. My only plans were to brush my teeth and lie down. Allen's book sat in my inbox. Why bother? Solving crimes wasn't my job, and the events of Amelia's Haven weren't my business. Hopefully, Paul's legal team knew what they were doing, and he'd be all right.

Or that's what I thought as I walked up the stairs with my laptop.

When I entered my room, the shiny new window reminded me that not everything was as it seemed in Amelia's Haven. Again, the feeling of unease, like someone had been here who didn't belong. Nothing was immediately obvious. My clothes were dumped out of my suitcase from my quick change en route to jail. Was that the problem?

I began refolding the clothes and putting them back. I was halfway through the stack when I picked up a piece of paper beside the sea chest. I was expecting the Mother's Day card I got Mom at the airport. Instead, what I held wasn't even paper. It was a napkin with a large seahorse printed on it. Red ink had been added, giving the seahorse a speech bubble. The seahorse was saying, *Srsly, drop it.*

Creepy.

Someone had not only thrown a brick through my window but then felt the need to add a murderous seahorse in my bedroom to ensure there was no confusion. What was their problem? Didn't they know I was retiring?

Should I call the cops? How would that conversation go?

*"Help police!"*

*"What's the problem?"*

*"I found a threatening napkin!"*

My detective friend would love that. Should I call just to annoy him?

When had the napkin been placed? Had I missed it when Dad and I checked out the new window? Or was it after dressing for prison? Was my scary seahorse warning me to take the brick seriously? Was it because I visited Paul? Or possibly my conversations with Dakota or Mr. FunRun's sister?

With such a busy day, it was hard to say for sure.

I wanted to return to the big house, make a cup of tea, and spend a second night on the living room couch. The problem was, Mom would be there and find out what was wrong. Sooner or later, she'd decide the threat was serious, and there'd be a big to-do with the boys in blue.

I decided the safest place for the seahorse napkin was under the sea chest, where its eyes wouldn't watch me. Why leave a threat for someone who's about to go to bed? I'd *srsly* been about to *drop it* for a good night's sleep, but this napkin litterer had to go and ruin it with a threat.

Time to read Allen's book. Nothing like a little true crime before bed. Getting settled on the couch with my computer, I found the email sitting between promotional spam for engraved cuff links (don't ask) and muscle tees (I'm shredded). Opening the document, I expected it to read like a juicy tell-all. Allen had to know who killed him.

Super energized, I was ready to unmask Allen's monster.

Then I started reading.

The writing style had the prose of someone who'd kept their day job and only fulfilled their dream of writing in retirement. Three pages in, I yawned one of those jaw-splitting, eye-watering yawns. So far, all he'd gotten to was describing what the beach looked like. I began skimming. Why couldn't he start the story with who killed him? Page five, he'd made it to Amelia's Haven, detailing the shops, the locals, and the tourists. Even at this faster pace, I was still dying and moved to sit on the floor, hoping the less comfortable seat would keep my eyes open.

In high school, Casey forced me to watch every episode of *Friends* when we both had mono. You remember that episode where Rachel has written like forty pages of feelings, and Ross falls asleep partway through reading and accidentally agrees the two of them *weren't* on a break, and he cheated? That's what reading Allen's first draft was like. It was a single-spaced nightmare.

Finally, on page twenty-seven, the crime portion of the true crime began. Actually reading now, I went through each sentence of Allen's sawdust compositions, ready for any kind of clue. At first it seemed a big waste, and I caught my head nodding toward the keyboard more than once. Allen explained how the mansion looked at sunset and what DJ's final thoughts must have been as he succumbed to death…in the most mundane way possible. Instead of DJ Hughes being on the cusp of some great masterpiece, as millions of influencers suggested, Allen had him looking out on the beach and thinking, *I like to surf. So I hope tomorrow is a good set of waves for surfing. Because I came here to unwind and surf, as I told* People *magazine in their previous issue.*

Yikes.

But then came a section with a picture attached—one I'd forgotten I'd seen—of Dakota in handcuffs.

According to Allen, Dakota had been arrested regarding DJ's case. She'd been taken to the station before getting released three hours later. After that, Dakota and my favorite detective became inseparable.

The story continued with how the manager was caught and all the press that followed. It caused a boom in Amelia's Haven tourism, which Allen detailed and I ignored.

At the end of the DJ Hughes section was a random sentence. It stuck out since everything else had been straightforward prose—if you could call his writing that. *Dakota and Reynolds weren't seen together in the weeks following the close of DJ Hughes's case.* Made sense. I couldn't quite picture what the relationship between the officer and the landlady was like. Were they ever lovey-dovey?

DJ's murder was the only completed story. On the following pages, the other murders had varying levels of notes and paragraphs strung together. The murder poem jumped out on a page:

> The manager's anger turned red,
> DJ Hughes was found dead
>
> Jeremy lay in Corpse Pose,
> From which he never rose

# A NOT SO SHOCKING MURDER

> When the phone cord went tight,
> The councilwoman saw the light
>
> Binoculars for birding,
> Found a new use for hurting
>
> A trident's bite,
> To end someone's night

It was missing the final verse with brewing and spewing. A part of me wanted to add it in. Would Allen be honored he was included?

There was an overwhelming amount of information about the birdwatching murder that kept Allen in Amelia's Haven. But it was all notes. Quotes from random people involved. Plus timelines, so many timelines. Allen detailed where he was. Where his friend was. Where his friend's murdered girlfriend was.

The section surrounding Britt's fiancé was beginning to take shape. The basics of the case were covered. But there were a lot of other pieces that didn't tie together. In the first paragraph, I found out Jeremy was in the coast guard. Which is just fantastic. Brittany didn't just have some meditating yogic fiancé. He was also active military and (if Allen's to be believed) quite the hunk.

The most bizarre section read like an early draft for *Mean Girls*, detailing Brittany's life in high school. At first I assumed it was part of Allen's extensive background research on Jeremy's friends and family. Then Dakota showed up, and I read about a prank. It had to be the one Paul referenced. The event was so much worse than pouring juice on someone's shorts.

From what Allen said, Brittany had always been a step or two ahead of Dakota. Getting better grades, having more friends, and being the best at any extracurricular she set her mind to. Dakota decided Brittany should be punished for her good fortune. She forged letters between Brittany's dead dad and a math teacher full of scandalous details about an affair and passed copies around the school.

Dakota's revenge blew up in her face. The forgeries were quickly discovered. Britt's dad had been dead before the Asatos moved into town, and it wasn't long before it all traced back to Dakota. She became the most hated person in high school. Even the parents of the other teens gave her a wide berth. Paul had been gone on a school trip, but after returning, he punched a dent in Dakota's locker, warning her to never mess with Brittany again. It got so bad Dakota finished high school in Carentorrie and avoided the entire town of Amelia's Haven for years. She moved back a few months before the DJ Hughes murder, when she returned to manage the family rental business.

That was all kinds of messed up. What was Dakota's problem? I've pulled plenty of pranks in my life, but nothing close to faking an affair involving someone's dead dad.

Allen's words circled back to Jeremy's murder and the suspects' alibis. He spent extra time detailing how the mayor's heart attack kept Britt from meeting Jeremy and how Paul, alone on his boat, had the weakest alibi. Pretty soon everything was stacking up against him, and he was found on his boat after apparently kidnapping Dakota.

Allen went over the details of his interview with Paul, but there was nothing I hadn't already heard from Paul. While Allen never came out and said it, from how he wrote, Allen didn't think Paul was guilty.

Next to Paul's arrest was written: *Evidence beyond circumstantial?*

Allen had still been researching the later murders. But what was his focus? What had he discovered that got him killed?

There were lots of notes throughout Jeremy's chapter. *Did Brittany really love Jeremy?* I stared at that one longer than I should've. Jeremy's murder had been two summers ago. Even if Brittany had loved him, had enough time passed for her to start seeing other people?

Allen's final notes in the section were about Dakota and Brittany. Whatever he'd been arguing with Dakota about at The Dining Seahorse, he definitely hadn't been talking about his lease. Allen was a reasonable guy. He wouldn't have gotten so upset about not getting his lease extended. Dakota had lied. But supposedly Dakota couldn't have killed Allen. She hadn't been in the diner long enough to poison him. I'd also seen her surprise when Allen collapsed. Miss Apricots wasn't that good an actress.

In that case, it left…No, it couldn't be…Was it…Brittany? Would she really be okay with Paul taking the fall? I remembered how the color had left Britt's face when I suggested some of the crimes were linked. Was she afraid I was on her trail? When she'd asked if I was willing to see Paul, I'd taken it as a friendly warning. Had it been a threat?

# CHAPTER 17

"Are you all right?"

I groaned. Cold hands were touching my bare skin. "Come on, Holt, wake up."

Was Mom in my room? Beginning to pry open my eyes, I immediately squeezed them shut. It was unimaginably bright out.

"Why are you on the floor?"

Was I on the floor?

"Did something happen?"

More zombie than human, even I found my answer unintelligible. When I pushed myself up, my hand found something wet. Finally opening my eyes, I could see my hand was in an alarmingly big puddle of drool.

"Are you okay?"

Mom had started over-enunciating. Super.

"I'm good." My voice was full of gravel.

My mother pursed her lips in the universal mom sign of disapproval. "It's almost time for Whaling with Wally."

I squinted. The day hadn't started, and I already had a headache. "Isn't whaling illegal?"

Mom pursed her lips even tighter.

I was really batting a thousand. Happy Mother's Day Eve.

"We're not actually whaling. It's what Wally calls his whale-watching tours."

I opened my mouth, then shut it. My views on whale watching wouldn't be appreciated. Mom also wouldn't want to hear my suspicions of the whale watcher guide's name being something other than Wally. So I tried a more practical question. "Do I have time to shower?"

"If you hurry. I'll get you oatmeal in a to-go cup."

Fantastic.

---

We boarded the same multilevel tour boat as we had the day before. The sky was gray and the ocean was calm. After chugging out to sea, the boat stopped. At first I worried we'd broken down again. But this was supposed to happen. We would float there, dead in the water, hoping whales would appear.

It was the same boat, but Mom had neglected to mention that Whaling with Wally was a weekend attraction for families. Saturday morning, the boat was filled with at least fifteen other families, with too many brats to count. The boat was so noisy. Happy screams mixed with angry and sad screams until screaming echoed all over with no escape. Had I been warned, I would have brought my noise-canceling headphones. Yesterday's secluded spot was now occupied by a mom whose kid was battling seasickness.

Casey found me huddled behind a lifeboat on the top deck. I hadn't stopped stewing about Brittany possibly being a murderer since Mom had scraped me off the floor.

Her eyes darted from me to the surrounding area. "Have you seen Baxter?" she asked.

I shook my head. Then, because I'm a selfless uncle, asked, "Do you want help?"

"Oh, hold on." Casey looked down at the lower deck. "He's with Juniper."

"Super."

Casey gave me a look. How sarcastic had I sounded? Time to sound like the loving uncle everyone knew I was. "You know, after thirty-seven minutes lost at sea with this band of ruffians, I can honestly say your kids aren't so bad."

Casey actually looked surprised. "That's one of the nicest things you've ever said."

I rested my hand on her arm. "And I meant it."

She rolled her eyes. "Don't go soft on me now."

"Wouldn't dream of it."

As Casey left, my thoughts returned to stewing about Jeremy's murder. Was his death the start of something? The later deaths in Amelia's Haven were almost showing off. The acts of someone who would throw a brick through my window.

What made DJ Hughes's murder interesting was the fact it was a celebrity. Strip that away, and all you have is a dude pushing another dude down the stairs. That kind of murder has been happening since staircases were invented.

The later ones were different. They were created to be sensational. How else would you have the opportunity to kill someone in a phone booth? And who used a trident as a murder weapon? Even the poisoning had happened in a crowded restaurant with security cameras. Way different from the simple shove DJ got.

"Quite the face you've got there." It was Casey. Hadn't she left?

"I'm pretty sure an innocent man is behind bars."

"At your work? Fraud or something?"

What work? Whose fraud? My confusion lasted only a couple of seconds. "Not work. Here. I think the fisherman didn't do it. It'd be great if it could be the annoying rental agent—"

"Dakota?"

"—but I'm worried it's the fisherman's sister. I'm not sure why. And I don't know how. But it kind of has to be her. She's too perfect. A mirage."

Casey had been serious during the first part of my speech, but her expression changed when Brittany came up. "Did you call a woman a mirage?"

"No!"

"You did. Were you shot by Cupid's arrow? I've heard he likes those returned."

I ran a hand through my hair. "Wow, thanks for the advice, sis. Really, top-notch."

"Wait, do you like her? Like, beyond someone to flirt with?" When my only reply was a grimace, Casey asked, "Can you exonerate the fisherman without a new arrest?"

"No."

"Okay." She thought about it. "Well, are the police still looking into it?"

"No."

Casey tried again. "Do you have any proof it's your perfect woman beyond the fact that she's perfect?"

"No."

"Have you talked to her about it?"

"No."

Casey made the same face she had when Baxter put her hairbrush in the toilet. "Not to downplay any of your accomplishments. But either you'll need to start figuring things out or prolong your vacation. We're scheduled to leave after tomorrow's Mother's Day brunch."

I groaned. Since when had the week gone by so quickly? Also, why was there a fancy dinner tonight and a holiday brunch tomorrow? Even for my mom, that was extra.

Casey was watching me, looking too much like Mom for comfort.

"Yeah, fine." I sighed. "It would be good to ask Brittany a few more questions."

Casey took a step back. "Brittany? Your EMT? The murderous fisherman's sister is the woman from the beach?"

I shook my head. "I have no idea who you're talking about."

"Holt!" Her eyes were big. "Don't hold out on me now!"

"Is that a whale?" I asked, pointing at nothing in particular.

Casey rolled her eyes, "You're no fun."

"I promised I wouldn't go soft."

---

By the time we docked, my stomach was lurching. This had more to do with being confined to a small space with miniature humans than being at sea. I was the first one off and took advantage of my long legs to make it as far from the evacuating families as possible.

My family was sheepdogged into the herd and shuffled off the ramp and across the pier with everyone else. Mom and Dad were the first ones to join me. Juniper and Jude would have come in second, except Juniper found the perfect spot for a selfie. Probably with a boring caption, like, LET'S BE MERMAIDS! As it was, Casey's entire family made it over before Juniper found the right filter.

"Water-horsey!" Baxter yelled (not screamed) in excitement (not rebellion). Still annoying. But on day five of our *awesome family vacay*, I was learning to take the silver linings where I found them.

Casey gave Mom a look. "As you know, Baxter hasn't eaten much. The only thing he found acceptable was the mac 'n' cheese at The Dining Seahorse. I told him our family would eat there for lunch. You're all welcome to join us, or we can meet up after."

Baxter wasn't eating? Since when? If he spent less time spilling on me and more time eating, his problems would be solved.

"Would you go back?" Mom asked me.

I shrugged, deciding it was best not to volunteer the fact I'd already been back.

"We'll all go to The Dining Seahorse," Mom decided as Juniper and Jude joined us.

"The dead guy restaurant?" Jude asked. Were those his first words all trip?

"Is that a problem?" Mom asked.

"We're good to go," Juniper answered. Well, at least Jude got four words out on this trip. They say women marry their fathers, but Juniper took it to an extreme. I was surprised Jude could cough up an *I do* at their wedding—let alone say the vows.

Going into the *water-horsey* restaurant that had creeped me out before a man had dropped dead didn't help my stomach. Settling on water and an order of fries, I did my best to keep from drumming my fingers on the table as everyone else ate their food.

Baxter was partway through a second helping of mac 'n' cheese (identical to the kind from a Kraft box) when I slid out my phone and discreetly checked notifications. A new email from Allen's sister was sent almost two hours ago.

It read: *Went by Allen's. Office ransacked. Police came. Are asking about his book.*

A photo was attached, showing papers strewn and a shattered laptop.

Seriously? Amelia's Haven was the absolute armpit of society.

If Allen's book had been a secret before, the cat was officially out of the bag. Did the thief know I'd read the book? For all the good it did. Allen really should have written a few more notes before getting murdered.

All of a sudden, my leg was kicked. I assumed Juniper was alerting me of Mom catching my unscheduled phone time. Unlike Jude, I can't play on my phone all day. Instead, it was Casey jerking her head toward the window. There was Brittany, exiting the post office in shorts and a light sweater. I swallowed, all too aware Casey watched as I debated what to do. Finally, I cleared my throat, tossed my napkin on the table, and stood. "Excuse me," I said before exiting.

"Britt," I called, forgetting to look both ways as I crossed the street. A car honked and swerved. If I hadn't had her attention before, I certainly had it now.

Brittany's face turned serious for an instant, but by the time I made it to her side of the street, her lips had a strange pull to them. She was trying to keep from laughing. "You almost got another ambulance called."

Running a hand through my hair, I decided to play it off. "Three in one week. Is that a record?"

A faint smile appeared as Britt replied, "I'd have to check."

There was silence. And I knew I was supposed to fill it.

Say something smooth like, *I was wondering, are you a murderer?*

She stood waiting. Her black hair was in a high ponytail, and those brown eyes were staring up at me. What was the proper way to interview a murder suspect? Did I bring up Dakota's prank? This would all be so much easier if Britt didn't smell amazing.

"Can I help you with something?" Britt asked.

How long had I been stuck in my thoughts?

"I had a question about…Allen."

"Oh." Brittany was confused and maybe disappointed. That couldn't be right. What would she be disappointed about?

"Not Allen. Sorry, I…" This wasn't working. I couldn't ask about her involvement in the middle of the street. Scratching the back of my neck, I tried a different route. "Would you drink with me? Or, get a drink with me?" I was an idiot. Why would she say yes? We'd known each other less than a week, I'd been a total mess of a human being every time she saw me, plus I was leaving tomorrow. These realizations only kept me talking. "Not right now, but at five. We could go to The Marina and—"

"I'd prefer The Dining Seahorse."

Glancing back at that cursed restaurant, I was met with my entire family (excluding Jude) plastering their faces to the window.

*Concentrate on Britt. Kill them later.*

Clearing my throat, I turned back. "Really? You'll go? Um, sure. Wherever you want."

I would have hives being out with her regardless of the location. I could brave the creepy water-horsey joint one more time.

"Holt?" Britt's hand was on my arm.

"Hm?"

"I'm kidding. Five o'clock at The Marina."

"Yes. And I'll have to leave right at six. My mom has this big night planned, and after skipping the boat ride yesterday and it being Mother's Day Eve, I'll really be in the doghouse if I'm late. Also, there's a chance we'll get stuck in Watershed Gardens, and I'll be late. Five o'clock is scheduled as free time, but that doesn't always mean—"

"Holt," Brittany cut in.

"Yes?"

"Stop talking."

"Okay."

Her eyes sparkled as she walked away.

While I would never admit this to my family, I felt my stomach give a sickening flip. Murderer or not, I had a date tonight.

# CHAPTER 18

The afternoon's itinerary was blessedly quieter than the morning's Whaling with Wally. Watershed Gardens was a huge beachside garden, and all we were supposed to do was stroll through it.

While there were palm trees instead of pine, this was the best of all the outings Mom had planned. As long as we were there, I could almost pretend I wasn't next to some infernal beach—though the scents and the sounds of the ocean were ever-present.

I had separated from the group and was looking for a quiet place to sit and figure out what to ask Britt when Juniper and Casey caught up with me.

"We were just talking," Casey said. "Are we supposed to give our Mother's Day gifts tonight or tomorrow at brunch?"

"Gifts?" I asked.

Casey and Juniper shared a look.

"What did you bring Mom?" asked Juniper.

"I brought myself."

Casey tsked.

"And a card," I added.

Casey shook her head. "It's fine. Yesterday I bought a scarf Mom would really like. I was saving it for her birthday, but it can be from Holt."

I slid my sunglasses a little higher up my nose. "This isn't necessary. Mom got all her descendants to press pause on their lives for a mandatory vacation. Us coming should be enough."

Neither sister answered but waited like they expected a punchline. When I didn't say anything else, Juniper turned to Casey. "Great. Holt can give Mom the scarf. And let's wait till tomorrow. Mom would want us to celebrate on the real day."

With that, my sisters were gone. I grabbed at my hair. Had *Holt gets ambushed* been scheduled?

Heading in the opposite direction of the ocean and my sisters, I came to a section that was almost overgrown, that had an inviting bench.

My stomach was a mess. Eating french fries for lunch hadn't solved the unease from the boat. And the discomfort had only increased after I asked Brittany out. I was about five minutes away from a bathroom emergency.

Brittany had been so adamant Paul was innocent. Was that because she was the killer? My stomach roiled at the thought.

Could I just let this go? Leave it up to the police and lawyers? That had been my plan last night. I could have a fun date with a stunning woman before skipping town. Then return to work and…reality?

It had to be Britt. I knew it. She'd killed Allen because he was close to discovering her secrets. He'd visited Paul. Had they driven to Carentorrie together? Who knows what Allen could have learned in two hours alone with her.

If it wasn't Britt, who was left? It wasn't me. Dakota hadn't been in the restaurant during the poisoning time frame. Bea was a teenage waitress. My detective friend was just a bully with an inflated ego. And Soccer Dad was probably too worried about his kid's game.

Could I leave tomorrow without knowing what happened? Could I forget Allen lying by a seahorse mural?

"You need a nap, old man," Dad said, startling me.

"Something like that," I said.

Dad sat next to me with a sigh. A tattered book appeared in his hand seconds later.

"New book?"

"It's *The Tenant of Wildfell Hall*." Dad settled on the bench. "I finished *The Maltese Falcon* last night."

I yawned. Why had he mentioned naps? The distant lapping of waves was perfect white noise for a drowsy afternoon. I had to snap out of it. "What happened in your book?"

He didn't reply.

"Dad, your falcon book's like a hundred years old. I've had my whole life to read it."

He shrugged. "Spade finds out the woman he's fallen in love with killed his partner in cold blood. Even though Spade loves her, he turns her in. She gets hanged, and his best friend can't stand the sight of him."

"Huh. That's…unfortunate."

My stomach gurgled. This was a different century. Different circumstances. If I proved Brittany's guilt, she wouldn't be doomed to a hangman's noose. Still, I shouldn't have asked.

"You have something nice to wear tonight?"

"Hm?" At first I thought he meant for my date, but then I remembered Mom's formal dinner. Would the family secret be revealed then? "Yeah. I packed something special."

"Good."

Dad opened his book, already a few chapters in. Was he frailer? More wrinkles? Whiter hair?

"Are you and Mom going to tell us something tonight?"

"Your mother's too old to be pregnant."

"Dad!"

He sighed. "No," he said simply. "Not tonight."

"But tomorrow?"

All I got was a head tilt.

---

Dad and I both conked out on the bench, sagging into each other like the old men from The Muppets. Before waking us up, Mom and Juniper took plenty of photos to memorialize the moment. A little freaky to see. With our features relaxed, I was a twenty-years-younger replica of Dad. Have I mentioned Dad's extremely attractive?

"I'll caption this one, LIKE FATHER, LIKE SON," Juniper said, shoving her phone in my face for the seventeenth time since we'd gotten in the van.

I yawned. "Can we get some coffee?"

Dad yawned at the steering wheel. "Do we have time?"

Mom laughed. "We'd better get it on the schedule. I don't want either of my men nodding off into the soup."

The triple-shot iced latte did its job in reviving me. I almost felt ready for my upcoming night when we got to the beach house. Though with the impromptu nap, I still hadn't figured out what I would ask Brittany.

After showering to wash off any whale residue, I planned on googling interrogation tactics. As brilliant as my googling plan was, it didn't account for how long it took me to get ready.

Drinks on the beach, while a date, is much less formal than the dinner Mom was dragging us to. So for the date, I decided on my gray slacks and a canvas button-up shirt with rolled-up sleeves and the top couple of buttons undone. Then, between drinks and dinner, I'd unroll the sleeves, add cuff links, button up the shirt, add a tie, and top it off with the suit jacket. Two killer looks in one killer evening.

I was fixing my hair when footsteps on the stairs hit me. A cold sweat broke out. Was it Brittany canceling? Dakota with more questions? It was Juniper.

Frowning, I tried to look unwelcoming. Hadn't she reaped the rewards of me being delightful for the past few days?

"Show's over, ladies and gentlemen," Juniper announced, not at all bothered about joining me in the cramped bathroom while I fixed my hair. "You don't need to go home, but you can't stay here."

"Something like that," I muttered.

Juniper didn't say anything else—though she was dying to. She probably hoped if I acclimated myself to her being there, I'd start talking when ready. Waiting for me to be ready would take the whole night.

Still, Juniper waited…and waited.

"A little birdie told me something," she finally said.

I didn't reply, unwilling to take the bait. The little birdie was Casey. Doubtless Juniper had heard all my suspicions about

Brittany while my sisters had walked through Watershed Gardens. All Juniper wanted was more dirt about my life.

Juniper gave a long-suffering little-sister sigh. "You know, I've never seen you like this. If anything with Brittany comes up, you look…happy."

"I'm always happy," I grumbled.

Juniper rolled her eyes. "My mistake." She huffed out a breath. "Just be careful. Don't accuse her of anything without proof."

I glared at Juniper's reflection in the mirror. "I'm getting proof. That's the only reason I asked her out."

"The only reason?" she asked skeptically.

"Yes, the only reason. The killer's Brittany. It has to be Brittany."

"Fine." Juniper shook her head like I was being difficult. She started to leave, then moved even closer and placed a tentative hand on my shoulder. "Be careful. I don't want you to ruin a chance with this woman because it's easier for you to believe she's a murderer than admit your feelings."

This was beyond anything I'd expected. I gave a slight nod signifying I heard. When I did speak, my voice was deeper than usual. "I don't have feelings."

"Then why does it have to be Brittany?"

"Because," I said.

"Because?" Juniper mimicked.

I was too busy white-knuckling the sink to reply.

Juniper pecked my cheek. "I'll go find Jude."

Rubbing my face, I tried to pull myself together. Stupid Juniper, this was all her fault. Britt had to be the murderer. Had to be.

# A NOT SO SHOCKING MURDER

While I'd never figured out what I would say to Brittany, I had managed to get to The Marina early—taking Dad's Corvette helped.

Britt was earlier. Sitting at the outdoor bar with a book in hand. She'd changed into a purple summer dress, was wearing strappy shoes, and had done something magical to her hair. She was already the hottest woman with her hair pulled back and wearing a paramedic uniform. But this…this was something else.

She hadn't spotted me. I was stuck where I stood, staring at her like a creeper. My throat had gone dry. I tried to swallow, but my mouth was too dry. Smoothing out my hair, I discovered a tremor in my hands.

Managing to move my feet forward, I finally made it to Britt. In my mind, I was going to say something smooth, using buzzwords like *breathtaking* or *stunning*. However, that would require a functioning brain or a mouth that wasn't drier than the Sahara. What came out of my mouth when I finally croaked out sound was "Wow."

If the sight of Britt had wrecked my brain, her taking me in head to toe and blushing left me with an irregular heartbeat.

My eyes were unable to leave hers. I found my stool with my hands and managed to sit down without major embarrassment.

*I really like this woman.*

Could Juniper be right? Was I making up conspiracies to keep myself from liking a woman I was clearly nuts about? Tasha, my psych-major ex from college, said I had an avoidant attachment style. Whatever that means, it probably includes picking holes through potential mates to keep my distance.

Beyond my greeting, I hadn't said a word. I shook my head. "I'm sorry. It sounds like a line, but I'm speechless."

She winked—actually winked—and said, "There are worse things."

We ordered our drinks, and I was almost too enamored by Britt to care that my mojito came with a bright yellow umbrella—almost, but there are levels.

As we sipped our drinks, we began talking about *Die Hard*, of all things. Could I maneuver movie crimes into real-life ones? Trying to figure out how, while still midconversation with Britt, I made a joke she found so funny she threw her head back to laugh, and her neck was on perfect display. I don't know what it was about her neck... It's not like I have vampire fantasies. But I decided with absolute certainty that even if she did kill all those people, I didn't care. Paul could rot in Alcatraz.

There you have it. My detective days were over. So what if she was a killer? Wasn't that the deal with *The Maltese Falcon*? The dude's supposed to forget the lady's a cold-blooded killer and be with her anyway? I was willing to be that man. Besides, what proof did I have?

A headache began forming between my temples. Strange one would make an appearance on such a wonderful night. I took a gulp of my mojito, gagging mid-swallow. Now, a headache could just be a headache, but it could also be the first symptom of poisoning.

If Britt had killed Allen because of his true-crime piece, would she kill me for reading it?

It became clear at that moment that going for drinks with a suspected poisoner was about as stupid as the girl in the Geico commercials who wanted to hide behind chainsaws. My vision was growing blurry, and my throat was swelling.

"Holt, are you all right? You look a little green."

My eyes locked with the woman sitting beside me. She looked so innocent, even concerned. Britt deserved an Oscar for her acting.

"Um, no, I…" Even worse, looking into Britt's eyes had me forgetting I'd been poisoned. *Get it together, man. You're sitting next to a poisoner. Leave.* "Actually, I need to go wash up. Excuse me."

Trying not to stumble, I made it off the barstool as the sweats hit me. Was I dying? Could it be food poisoning from my fries at The Dining Seahorse—was Baxter my undoing? Glancing back at Brittany, I knew it wasn't a bad fry.

Zoinks, Scoob. I was really in for it.

Turning the corner from the outdoor bar, I pulled out my phone. If I called 911, would they just send Britt, and she could make doubly sure I didn't make it to tomorrow? Deciding my mom would know how to fix it, I was pulling up her name in my contacts—difficult to do with trembling fingers and blurred vision. Then I walked into someone.

Bouncing back, I squinted at the person. Was it really my detective friend? Could he actually be in the right place, at the right time, for the first time ever?

I blinked. "Excuse me." Or that's what I did my best to say. Whatever had happened to my throat had moved on to my tongue.

Why was I bothering with politeness? I needed help now.

"Does someone have your car keys?"

Swaying forward, I didn't bother insulting him. Instead, I managed to say, "Poisoned," as I stumbled into him again.

He let out a huge sigh, like I'd greatly inconvenienced him. "All right. Let's get you inside." He put an arm around me and began leading me toward The Marina's service entrance. "It looks like you got what Paul was given, not Allen. You should be fine. But we'll get you looked at."

Leading me through the entrance, my detective friend had to partially drag me down the hallway. At the door for a private dining room, the opening was too narrow for both of us. He let go of me and entered the room. Leaning against the doorframe, I blinked. Everything around me had slowed down. Something was wrong. Something didn't add up…If I could just remember whatever it was.

"Did you say Paul was drugged?" I garbled.

"I can't understand what you're saying. Come in where it's safe."

My thinker betrayed me, working way too slowly. I did as requested, stepping through the door.

There was a cracking sound against my head, and everything around me started getting brighter and brighter. Images began disappearing in the light, but I managed to look behind me. Dakota was hiding behind the door, holding a broken bottle in gloved hands. She quickly disappeared from view as the world got even brighter until everything was a piercing white.

My last thought before the brightness took me down was *Don't break your nose.*

# CHAPTER 19

Remember in movies when someone has been drugged or hit unconscious? When they start to wake up, they murmur or groan, effectively ruining any pretense of still being unconscious. Well, that has always driven me nuts. Sure, you're in pain and confused, but keep it together. Don't give up your one advantage of your captors thinking you're unconscious.

What did I do when I woke up with ankles zip-tied against the legs of a metal chair and my wrists zip-tied behind my back?

What I did was much smoother and debonair than moaning and groaning. I began choking, coughing, and spluttering. I hadn't exactly swallowed my tongue, but there was definitely saliva in places it didn't belong.

When I attempted to rub my eyes, I was reminded that my arms were bound. Through blurry eyes, I did my best to take in my surroundings. It all sounds so cliché, but I was actually being held in an abandoned building. There were gaps in the interior walls with plaster and wood sticking out. Rusted piping ran the course of the room. Instead of electricity, the room was lit by a couple of work lights, and the whole place smelled of rot and mildew. Was this where James Bond was tortured?

The first thing I focused on was hundreds of tiny bananas.

*Am I hallucinating?*

"Hello, sleepyhead." It was Dakota. The bananas were on Dakota's clothes. It all made sense.

I opened my mouth to say something witty, but a groan came out.

"Sorry," Dakota continued, circling the chair. I didn't follow her because my head was throbbing with all the glass she'd smashed into it. "This really was a communication failure. See, Reynolds decided to drug you and didn't tell me, so I thought I needed to incapacitate you when he brought you into the room. Doing both was…overkill."

"Yeah, well…" Again, I came up empty. Was this what a traumatic brain injury felt like?

I began pulling my wrists and legs against the zip cords. There was no give in the metal chair or the cords. Yet I kept tugging, even as cuts began forming on my wrists. I wasn't about to break free, but it was something to do. If murdered, a proper autopsy would show I'd been bound.

"Don't worry," she said, patting my shoulder. "It will all be over soon. If I had my way, you'd already be…but"—she giggled and bit her finger—"Reynolds insisted we wait."

A sudden wave of pain blurred my vision. I hung my head back and let out a moan. If my death was right around the corner, did it really matter if I was a big baby about how much pain I was in? It was so bad, all I wanted was my mommy.

I straightened. Mom. When I didn't show up for dinner, she'd look for me and wouldn't stop until I was found. *Keep Dakota talking. Stretch this out as long as possible. Get all the information you can.*

My vision was slightly double, I did my best to look at the real Dakota. I suddenly knew what Allen had figured out right before he keeled over at The Dining Seahorse.

"You did them together? You and the cop?"

Dakota laughed. "Where's the fun in that? Rarely together. More like creating a puzzle for the other one to solve."

"So you didn't kill Allen? When Allen figured out you were the yoga murderer, he told your cop boyfriend, who took care of the problem."

"Isn't he thoughtful? Reynolds had him poisoned before I knew there was a problem. I was surprised as anyone when he fell over."

At least I was right about that instance of Dakota being innocent. I'd been wrong suspecting Brittany. But that meant I didn't have a crush on a murderer. This was a rare example of a time I was glad to be wrong.

"Was there something about DJ Hughes's murder that made you decide to kill?"

Dakota was impressed. "So you know we didn't kill him? Very good." She went to pat my head before remembering the mess she'd created in my hair. "That case was when I first met Reynolds. I'd just returned home, and he was newly transferred to Amelia's Haven Police. I didn't like him until he arrested me and…" Dakota giggled.

*What was with her?*

"…he interrogated me. It's really fun when he interrogates you."

Ew.

"I was exonerated, and we started working together like I was his informant or something. All those long nights working together, drinking cocoa, and our legs touching under the table were magical. Then, when the case was closed, it was like I didn't matter anymore, and he moved on with his life—without me."

"So you murdered Jeremy?"

"Well, it had worked the first time."

I rolled my eyes and muttered, "If it ain't broke."

Dakota didn't notice. "In a way, it was a murder of convenience. There Brittany was, waltzing around town like she was so much better than me. Like she was this little princess with perfect hair, and she'd found her Prince Charming. They were going to literally sail away together. It was all supposed to point back to her, but then she had to stumble upon a heart attack."

Was Dakota standing there, complaining about her bad luck?

"I was scrambling, but at least Reynolds was back, and we were working the case, getting hot cocoa and tracking down the fake leads I'd devised. He didn't tell me he'd figured it out. Do you know what he did?" She sighed. "He's so romantic. Reynolds figured out how to frame someone else, so I wouldn't be arrested. He drugged and kidnapped Paul, then kidnapped me to stage the scene. I didn't know what was happening until I'd been"—she made air quotes with her fingers—"'rescued.' We started dating after that. When we got in a rut a few months later, Reynolds strangled a councilwoman in the town's last phone booth. That way I had a case to solve. Every relationship needs a little excitement from time to time."

"Um…" I had no response. This had to be the weirdest relationship I'd ever witnessed. My mind strayed back to her first murder. "Why arrest Paul?"

She shrugged. "That was Reynolds's decision. Probably something boring, like Paul had the weakest alibi. It upset Brittany, so it worked for me."

This really wasn't the time to get angry or defend Britt…or that's what I kept telling myself as my body went rigid with fury.

"Why do you hate her so much?" My voice was low—maybe too low.

Dakota looked me over. "I see. She got you too." Dakota huffed—like she expected me to take her side. "Being a kid was great. I was popular and had all these friends. Then, in middle school, Brittany and Paul moved to Amelia's Haven because their dad died, and their mom wanted to be closer to family. All of a sudden, Brittany's there, and everyone feels sorry for her and thinks she's perfect. She gets everything for years!" Dakota's voice had grown shrill. "When I play one teeny-tiny prank to take her down a little, everyone acts like I'm some supervillain, and I have to switch schools, all because of her!"

I wished I could rub my temples. Everything Dakota spouted made my head throb worse.

A door slammed, and my cop friend walked in.

"Almost ready," he said.

At his entrance, Dakota perked right up. "Great."

Not great.

"What's the plan here?" I tried to gesture with my hands—to be reminded for the twenty-third time my hands were bound behind my back.

My cop friend came over to where I'd been tied up. My head was lolling to one side, and he squatted to meet my eyes.

"You don't remember? You and Allen go way back. He found out about your embezzling and told you to meet him in Amelia's Haven once he got enough proof. You came, and instead of striking a deal, you killed him."

I closed my eyes, a wave of dizziness hitting.

"Don't pass out," the detective said, hitting my cheeks. "We're almost at the fun part."

Groaning, I met his eyes again. "That won't hold up. I haven't been stealing."

The detective grinned. "Who's going to check? I'm the detective here, and I say you killed Allen and skipped town. No one will ever find your body. You'll disappear, just like Allen's birdwatching friend."

"Okay." I tried to make sense of this new information. "So, you killed Allen's friend and made it look like he was on the run?" My hair flopped across my forehead, and I wanted to fix it but couldn't. "You'll do the same thing for me because you don't have enough evidence. But for Paul, the phone booth strangulation, and the trident killing, you were able to fake enough evidence to make arrests."

"You're so good at this." Dakota applauded. "Can you guess who did which killing?"

This wasn't how I'd planned to spend my evening. "Um, I already know you did Jeremy." I took a deep breath, hoping extra oxygen would take away my dizziness. "Then your cop boyfriend killed the councilwoman."

"I'm a detective," my cop friend growled.

Dakota's eyes widened. "You really should treat him with respect."

"Why?" I asked as more hair fell into my face. "You'll kill me either way."

They didn't have a good answer to that one. How many murders were left? "Um, binocular bludgeoning, that sounds like something Dakota would do."

My cop friend's face was pure adoration as he said, "It sure is."

They were disgusting. But if they were distracted, they weren't murdering me. "Then I feel like Dakota would also like to use a trident."

"I did." Dakota's smile was dazzling. "I couldn't pass up a chance to use a trident."

Cool story.

"Then you're forgetting Allen's friend, who took the fall," Dakota said.

"Um…" I tried to choose between them. "I don't know. I don't know anything about that death."

"That was a fun one," Dakota said. "Reynolds did it; then I disposed of the body. Pretty soon he'll have you as a friend."

I laughed that annoying laugh that only happens in despair. "So I get you're going to kill me. The two of you have already killed what, like…?" My brain was too scrambled to count. "You've killed a lot of people. Don't let me waste your time with how I have a good life to live. I don't have kids, I'm not about to cure cancer, and a lot of people don't like me. Still, my mother will never believe I'm an embezzling killer who skipped town. She'll hire private investigators or call the governor." *Or break down this door any second…*

Dakota and the cop glanced at each other, not expecting my family's particular brand of crazy.

"Kill me and hide my body. My mother will find me. When I got an emergency appendectomy, Mom was ready with ice chips when I came out of surgery. Thing is, it was so rushed, I didn't tell her it was happening, and the hospital swears they never called. Don't know why she knew she had to hop on a plane or what hospital I was in, but that's the thing; she just knows."

Dakota looked over to her lover boy. "Kill them both?"

"Sounds like we have to."

They turned smug eyes on me.

Mom always said my mouth would get me into trouble. Guess she was right.

"That's one solution." I stalled, sweat forming at my temples. "Still, have you ever thought about getting some couples counseling or maybe taking a cooking class?"

My cop friend had a cocky smile, "Actually, I had something else in mind." Turning to Dakota, he took both her hands in his. "I love us so much."

Another wave of dizziness hit me as Dakota melted at his words.

"Whether it's your turn to plan a murder or mine, or we do it together, it's always fun, and I want this to keep going on forever." He got down on one knee as Dakota gasped.

*No, no, no, please, no.*

"I couldn't think of a better way to propose than here and now, doing what we love together." He let go of one of her hands and pulled out a ring box. "Dakota Willows, will you marry me?"

I'm not a delicate snowflake. I'm rarely shocked by the ways of the world. But this was extra.

She squealed, "Yes! Yes! Of course!"

What followed was gross smacking sounds until I blacked out.

# CHAPTER 20

"Now," my cop friend was saying as I regained consciousness. "Do you want to do this one by yourself or with me?"

Dakota patted his cheek. "You're so thoughtful. I've wanted to work on strangulation."

I began squirming, even though they were still yards away.

He winked. "I'll hold him still."

My cop friend stood behind me, his hands firmly on my shoulders. I was almost out of time.

As Dakota drew near, I asked, "Who threw the brick?"

"Me," my cop friend said.

Dakota covered her mouth. "That was a bit of an oopsie. Who knew you'd be sleeping on the couch?"

Was she serious?

"Did you expect me to sleep on that foldout?"

Dakota shrugged her shoulder.

Trying to keep the conversation going, I asked, "What about the napkin?"

Dakota raised her hand. "I left that. From what Reynolds said, you didn't take his threat seriously."

"And Allen's office?"

Dakota was about to answer when my cop friend shook my shoulders. "Quit stalling."

My eyes must have turned pleading because Dakota patted my knee. "Sorry, friend," she said. "Since you figured it out, you were the natural sacrifice."

Her hands moved to my neck. Her fingers almost tickled, lightly exploring as she played with my throat and veins. Then, when she nodded to her man, his grip tightened, and Dakota began to apply pressure.

"You know," I spluttered, trying to think of anything to buy more time. "I thought Brittany was the murderer."

The pressure released, and Dakota laughed. "That feels fun. Too bad for you. We've already committed. Any more last words?"

And my mind went blank. Seriously, why couldn't I think of anything to say when my life literally depended on it?

Taking my silence as a no, Dakota's hands began to tighten around my neck. I was going to be killed by someone dressed like a banana.

At the risk of being a horrible narrator, I'm not sure what happened next. One second Dakota and the cop were holding me down, pressing the life out of me. The next second the absolute worst sound I've ever heard was coupled with a flash brighter than the sun.

I could taste my brain.

I'd either gone deaf, or real sirens were going off. By the time I could make sense of this new round of double vision, big scary people with guns had Dakota and my detective friend on the floor in handcuffs.

Couldn't they have saved my life without using migraine-inducing explosives? My problems didn't end with the migraine. The explosion had done something to me. I was going to puke, and my arms and legs were still tied to a chair. While attempting to move my head away from my body, the chair tipped over with me still attached.

Next thing I knew, Brittany was there, cutting me free of the chair and doing a great job of ignoring the fact I was lying sideways next to a puddle of vomit. She might have told me to take it slow, but I still couldn't hear much beyond the ringing. Either the zip ties had cut off my blood flow, or the awful sound had wrecked my inner ear. As soon as I got to my feet, I fell over.

This was the absolute worst night of my life. First I thought a girl I really liked was a poisonous murderer and bailed on our date. Then, after I got kidnapped, she arrives with the cavalry and (yet again) witnesses me being a total mess of a human being.

Brittany and Soccer Dad began examining me, but I had to let Brittany know. My vision was still off, so it took a little while to figure out which swaying blob was her. Managing to grab her shoulder, I got her attention. "They did it. Killed your fiancé. Framed Paul. Everything after that was them too."

Brittany said something to Soccer Dad, and he gave us some space.

"I understand," I continued, "if you need to get some vigilante justice. No judgment here. But consider the prison time of taking matters into your own hands. Really think that through."

Bending down, so she was at eye level with me, Britt held my face with her gloved hands and started talking. This time I could hear—she was probably shouting. "Holt, first of all, everyone can hear you because you're yelling, so you took away my opportunity for a sneak attack. Second of all, I don't hurt people; I help them. Right now you need my help."

That was the second time I threw up.

Don't worry. Britt's years on the job made her a master of getting out of the way. Still humiliating.

Brittany had a cloth and began wiping up around my mouth. The scar by her eyebrow was visible, but a smile spread across her face. "Didn't you say puking was more of a second-date thing?"

*The woman is perfect.*

A hand on my shoulder made me start. It was my mother, who'd appeared out of nowhere. Her mouth moved, but all I got was ringing. So I started talking…or yelling. "I'm sorry I missed dinner."

Speaking at a volume I could hear, Mom said, "I'm glad you're safe. We can have my formal dinner next year."

I glared at Mom and almost puked for the third time.

Brittany and Soccer Dad began probing me while my ever-resourceful mother typed out the rescue mission's highlights on her phone—preferable to shouting for five minutes.

Basically, when I hadn't shown up at the house at 6:15 p.m., Mom went hunting. Not finding me in the garage, she got the details of my date from my sisters and went to The Marina.

Now, here's the crazy part—Brittany was still there. When I hadn't returned from the bathroom, she checked and found I wasn't there. She was standing in the parking lot by Dad's Corvette when Mom arrived.

At this point, Mom knew something was wrong and made a few calls—she probably knew the FBI director from Zumba.

She convinced people to bend a few rules and rescued me just in time.

By the end of this written explanation, my hearing had somewhat recovered—though the pounding in my head was still worse than the morning after my twenty-first birthday.

This was when Brittany informed me that my head was bleeding profusely from the broken bottle. "We're going to cut you out of your shirt to make sure the blood on your back is only from your head."

Brittany had the scissors in her hand, but she paused. For a second, the professional first responder was gone, replaced by a woman checking out her date. I'd planned on making a joke about her cutting me out of my clothes, but Britt's admiration made my stomach flutter and not in a puking way. Pulling Brittany down, so her ear was by my mouth, I did my best to whisper, "I have two more shirts like this one."

She laughed and rolled her eyes. "What a relief. This shirt won't be savable." And she cut my shirt off.

Touching her latex-gloved hand, I tried to look as sexy as a man who's just barfed twice can. "That purple dress you had on was terrific."

Britt's eyes sparkled. "Yeah?"

"Yeah, it's unforgettable. Even with…" I gestured toward the back of my head.

"That reminds me," Brittany said, eyeing my hair. "There's something else we have to cut off."

Mom put a hand on my shoulder as I looked between them. "You'd better say pants."

They didn't answer.

"You're not going to say pants."

Britt gave me a wink. "Don't worry, I used to cut my Barbie's hair all the time."

# CHAPTER 21

A traumatic saga followed as the scissors made horrible snipping sounds, leaving my glorious hair shorn into patchy sections that were almost bald in places. Mom holding my hand during the process was a little much—but I didn't let go.

I may have blacked out again. It's a little fuzzy. I remember getting loaded into an ambulance. Soccer Dad drove while Mom and Brittany sat on either side of my gurney. We were going to the Carentorrie hospital. Quite the drive to get to a properly equipped ER.

At the risk of sounding even more like a diva, my head really hurt, and it's not like the rest of me felt fantastic, either.

"Why is it whenever you need an ambulance, you're covered in glass?" Britt asked.

I blinked up at her. This was probably part of her training to distract patients, but I went along with it. "To be fair, the first time, I was sleep-deprived, dehydrated, and in shock. No glass was involved."

Britt shook her head. "My bad."

The vehicle hit a pothole, and the jerking left me grunting in pain—though I tried to stay silent with Brittany right there.

Mom patted my shoulder, and suddenly I'd had it. I was done with tiptoeing around, wondering what was wrong with Mom and Dad. Waiting and guessing and waiting some more.

"Mom?"

She bent close to my face like I was whispering. Was I whispering?

"Yes, honey?"

"What's the deal? I've tried to be patient, but I can't take it anymore. Are you or Dad dying, divorcing, retiring…buying a zoo?"

Confusion filled my mother's face. "What are you talking about?" She glanced over at Brittany like I was delirious.

"The trip. This trip. I'm sure you wanted the family all together to tell us something big."

"Oh." At first she was relieved I'd proven to have a strong hum in the drum. Then Mom frowned. "We were going to give you all the news tomorrow at the Mother's Day brunch on the beach."

Was she really going to hold out on me now? I was riding in an ambulance, stretched out on a gurney, headed for the hospital.

Moaning, I let my eyes roll back. It was over the top, and Mom knew it. Still, she took the hint.

"Fine. Since you might be missing brunch and eating hospital pudding instead, I'll tell you early, but no whispering it to Juniper. This stays in the ambulance. Okay?"

My eyes miraculously opened. "Mm-hmm."

"Your dad and I had been feeling unmotivated in life and not sure what we should be doing when a woman your dad went to college with contacted us to say—"

Wait, was she saying...? Did I have a half brother? Could the guy be married? Were there a few more nieces and nephews running around?

Mom had continued talking while my mind wandered. "...offering us both jobs at the University of Melbourne. We accepted and will be moving to Australia this July."

I lifted my head. "That's it?"

"Yes."

"You're moving to Australia?"

"Yes."

"That's crazy. Like I was almost murdered tonight, but this, this is the crazy part."

She swatted my arm. "Holt!"

I lay back. Learning my parents' problem was as simple as a joint midlife crisis was more of a relief than I expected. Sighing, I relaxed as much as possible and let my eyes close. "Mom?"

She took my left hand in both of hers. "Yeah?"

I cracked an eye open. "If you get a kangaroo, can I name it?"

"Absolutely not."

Groaning, I tried to look as awful as possible.

"Nice try. But there's no way you'll name any of our kangaroos."

She was giving me an opening to ask *How many kangaroos?* But I was too tired. So I said, "Yes, ma'am."

Mom kept holding my hand, and after a while I felt Brittany's gloved hand take my other hand. I squeezed her hand and grinned when she squeezed back.

Amelia's Haven wasn't so bad after all.

# SEATTLE

So, the worst part of rescuing Amelia's Haven from their hot-cocoa-making killer was I had to prolong my stay in that foul town. Mom ended up renting rooms for us at the haunted doll B and B and stayed with me until I was well enough to travel.

Do you have any idea how many people I had to talk to? So many things needed to be signed. All of it explaining the junk Dakota and her boy toy confessed to. Very, very important legal things that lawyers needed to get innocent people out of jail. A pain under normal circumstances, but I had to do it with a head injury. And trying to remember their specific words was about as easy as remembering what I'd had for lunch two months ago.

I left Amelia's Haven as soon as I was healthy enough to travel. It was such a relief to finally leave Oregon. Mom had wanted to come back to Seattle with me, in case I couldn't take care of myself. But I flat-out refused. Mom promised she'd sleep on the couch, like my only concern with her visit was losing mattress privileges. As great as my mother is, we'd had enough bonding time.

Considering I was successfully working, eating, and showing up to doctors' appointments, Mom needn't have worried.

My phone buzzed as I entered the parking garage from the doctor's office. I assumed it was Mom, sensing my stitches had been removed.

Her texts weren't exactly urgent, but the quicker I replied, the quicker I didn't need to worry about it. When I unlocked my phone, a telltale grin pulled at my mouth. The text wasn't from Mom but from Britt.

Brittany: *How'd it go?*
Me: *Still bald. Thx.*

I sent her a selfie of me wearing one of my many new hats.

Beyond the fact I have awesome hair and would never choose a buzz cut, there was also the visual of healing gashes that no one needed to see. Thank you, Miss Apricots.

After the pic, I added: *Appointment went well. Stitch-free. No more follow-ups.*

I immediately regretted pressing send. Not only had I spammed her with two texts and a photo, but I hadn't meant to tell her I had no more appointments.

Brittany took two whole minutes to reply: *That hat's my favorite.*

It was a beanie. I'm not usually a beanie person, but it was more comfortable than the other options. On a day when a nurse was poking around my head, I'd chosen comfort over style. Did Brittany actually like it best? I could become a beanie person.

Resisting the urge to ask follow-up questions regarding the beanie, I got into my car and reminded myself I was a level-headed grown-up.

Staring down at my phone, I debated what I should say. Then I remembered this was a big day for Brittany too.

Me: *Has he been released yet?*

Buckling up, I waited to turn on the car, willing Britt to send another text. An image downloaded. She'd sent a candid pic of her and Paul. They were sitting side by side at the burger joint we'd gone to in Carentorrie. Britt was positively beaming in the photo, so glad to have her brother back. Paul, on the other hand, was busy devouring a cheeseburger. After almost two years in jail, his first stop was for burgers. I knew I liked Paul.

A more mature person would have said something boring like, *Glad the paperwork went through.* While a less mature person would have made an arrogant comment about being the reason Paul was a free man. I settled for something in the middle.

Me: *Glad Paul's reconnecting with his true love.*

Britt sent back the crying-laughing emoji.

I stared down at my phone. Was that it? Could I reply to a single emoji? When nothing new appeared, I turned on the car.

I wanted to talk to Britt. It'd been so long since I'd heard her voice. She'd visited me in the Carentorrie hospital and then at the B and B. The excuse we'd settled on for exchanging numbers was so she could check on my health and I could find out about Paul's release.

In one day Paul had been released and I'd had my final appointment. With no more excuses, would we stop texting?

Would she want to talk? I'd never missed hearing someone's voice before. What was happening?

When I shifted into reverse, my phone buzzed, and I quickly had the car in park.

Brittany: *I told them your joke. Paul thought it was hilarious…His girlfriend was less amused.*

My fingers hovered above the keyboard. Was it weird to ask about calling?

At first I sent a sunglasses emoji. Then, trying not to overthink it, I added: *Are you free sometime for a phone call?*

After that I had to lock my phone. I couldn't watch the message get delivered. Couldn't stare at the dots as she typed her reply. Was I about to hyperventilate?

My phone lit up the moment I set it down. My heart was galloping as I unlocked the screen. Did Brittany want to keep me in her life?

*What?!*

Instead of her, it was Mom choosing the absolute worst time to ask about my appointment. My hand squeezed the phone so hard the plastic threatened to break. I couldn't think, let alone drive. I was trapped in a parking garage, held hostage, waiting for Brittany's answer.

A new text arrived. With a sinking feeling, I opened the message.

Brittany: *How's tomorrow night?*

I yelled and raised my arms like I'd won a gold medal.

Me: *Tomorrow's perfect.*

After that, I could appreciate Mom's text and the fact Brittany had asked about my appointment first.

Grinning, I sent Mom: *I'm good.*

Then added: *The appointment ended ten minutes ago...You're losing your touch.*

———◆◯◆———

What does a burglary, a borrowed dog, and burnt onions have in common? Read Holt's next mystery *A Not So Rustic Retreat* to find out.

Want to know what happened to Holt at SEATAC airport before his flight to Amelia's Haven? Sign up for my newsletter at [lilystirling.com](lilystirling.com) and receive a copy of *Holt Jacobs & The Mystery Of The Missing Sunglasses.*

# Congratulations!

You just read an entire book!

I hope you enjoyed hanging with Holt and the entire Jacobs family as much as I do.

The idea for the story sparked when I was reading a small-town murder mystery while vacationing *in a small town*. It led to an interesting question. What would I do if I found out my little slice of heaven had a murder problem every few months?

Then (because it's me), I imagined I was a thirty-year-old man addicted to coffee.

Quite the stretch because I'm not thirty, a man, or addicted to coffee…okay, I might be slightly addicted to coffee, but not as bad as Holt.

If you *liked* Holt's first adventure, you should definitely check out his second mystery, *A Not So Rustic Retreat.*

Oh, and assuming you liked *A Not So Shocking Murder,* we should hang out. Go to *lilystirling.com* to sign up for my newsletter. You'll get to read *Holt Jacobs & The Mystery Of The Missing Sunglasses* plus receive my every-other-week updates.

There's no pot of gold at the end of this, just an author who's thrilled you made it here.

Until next time!

~ *Lily Stirling*

# About the Author

Lily Stirling has spent a quarter of a century living in the Pacific Northwest. She was born in Idaho, but her family moved to Washington around the time Lily could read chapter books.

Mysteries have always delighted her, from listening to *The Hardy Boys* on car trips to watching episodes of *Psych*.

As for sarcastic families, when she's not writing about one, she's living in one.

Mysteries are seldom fun to experience, but always fun to read or watch.

# Acknowledgments

Wow.

After so much sarcasm, will you actually believe me as I do a roll call for all the people who helped me create this book?

Imagine a woman's voice speaking very sincerely…whatever that sounds like.

---

I am so blessed to have such an excellent team working behind the scenes of this book. Each one of you is so talented, professional, and helpful. Thank you so much for working with me.

Production Team:

Developmental Editor ~ Kristen Weber

Copyeditor ~ Penina Lopez

Proofreader ~ Elaini Caruso

Cover Designer ~ Mariah Sinclair

---

Mom and Dad, thank you for the constant love and support you've given me my entire life. Also, for being my early readers and willing to share your thoughts—even when you both asked if I knew how bad my murder poem was.

To Melissa, thanks for always encouraging and believing in me more than seems rationally credible.

Dani, thank you for telling me what the Oregon Coast is like.

Huge thanks to my mom's friend, Jenny, for reading a draft and having honest and helpful suggestions.

Also, a big thank you to Alessandra Torre, Terezia Barna, and everyone at Inkers Con for all the priceless information. I'm so glad we found each other.

To Thomas Umstattd Jr. and James L. Rubart at Author Media/Novel Marketing podcast, thanks for all the wonderful help and advice.

Finally, thank *you* for taking the time to read my book and making it through the acknowledgments. Do you also watch movie credits? I know I do.

Thanks again!
Lily Stirling

Manufactured by Amazon.ca
Acheson, AB